William Shakespeare's The Tempest: A Retelling in Prose

David Bruce

Published by David Bruce, 2022.

WILLIAM SHAKESPEARE'S THE TEMPEST: A RETELLING IN PROSE

First edition. July 28, 2022.

Copyright © 2022 David Bruce.

ISBN: 979-8201453114

Written by David Bruce.

Table of Contents

Dedication

Dedicated to My Sister Brenda Kennedy

Brenda wrote, "During COVID and when visitors were restricted from visiting their loved one in the assisted-living facility I worked at, a patient mentioned to me how much she liked spaghetti during a late-night conversation we had. She was a night owl like me. Her name was Dee. I called her "Gerdy." Then she would say, "Dirty Gerdy," and we'd laugh. Anyway, on my way to work I bought two spaghetti meals from Olive Garden. I left for work early that night. I went to work, set up outlet dinners in the dining room, went to her room and wheeled her down to the dining room where we had dinner together. At that time, the residents weren't leaving their room and had their meals alone in their room. It was nighttime and everyone was already in bed, so I didn't see a problem. She was so grateful and had enough food for three more meals. It was such a simple gesture, but during that time it meant so much to her and for me."

Brenda once bought a newspaper at a gas station on Thanksgiving and tipped the female employee $5, and the employee cried.

Brenda wrote, "I do remember that. I also remember when George tipped a TeeJays waitress $100, and she cried. Our family does a lot of good deeds all the time: I unload people's grocery carts when the people are in those electric scooters. If they are alone with a few groceries, I'll leave cash for the cashier to pay for the groceries. I've had a lot of good deeds done to me when I didn't have a lot of money. It feels good to pay it forward."

She added, "I just have one more thing to add and then I'm done. I've had a lot of people in my life do good deeds for me when I was at a low point on my life. I was at a low point for a very long time. David, you know what you've done for me, and I can never thank you enough. Martha paid for antibiotics for me when I had strep throat and didn't have money. Rosa bought me groceries. Carla has done so much, and she had us over for Easter just after Chad died. When I say US, I mean all of my kids. She was so sick and ended up at the Emergency Room that same night. Frank gave me a car. And George buys my gas for me whenever he's in Florida. And Mom and Dad were good people. I had a lot of good influences in my life that made me be a good person. At least I hope I'm a good person. I try to be someone Mom and Dad would be proud of."

***

The doing of good deeds is important. As a free person, you can choose to live your life as a good person or as a bad person. To be a good person, do good deeds. To be a bad person, do bad deeds. If you do good deeds, you will become good. If you do bad deeds, you will become bad. To become the person you want to be, act as if you already are that kind of person. Each of us chooses what kind of person we will become. To become a good person, do the things a good person does. To become a bad person, do the things a bad person does. The opportunity to take action to become the kind of person you want to be is yours.

Educate Yourself
Read Like A Wolf Eats
Be Excellent to Each Other
Books Then, Books Now, Books Forever

***

In this retelling, as in all my retellings, I have tried to make the work of literature accessible to modern readers who may lack the knowledge about mythology, religion, and history that the literary work's contemporary audience had.

Do you know a language other than English? If you do, I give you permission to translate this book, copyright your translation, publish or self-publish it, and keep all the royalties for yourself. (Do give me credit, of course, for the original retelling.)

I would like to see my retellings of classic literature used in schools, so I give permission to the country of Finland (and all other countries) to give copies of this book to all students forever. I also give permission to the state of Texas (and all other states) to give copies of this book to all students forever. I also give permission to all teachers to give copies of this book to all students forever.

Teachers need not actually teach my retellings. Teachers are welcome to give students copies of my eBooks as background material. For example, if they are teaching Homer's *Iliad* and *Odyssey*, teachers are welcome to give students copies of my *Virgil's* Aeneid: *A Retelling in Prose* and tell students, "Here's another ancient epic you may want to read in your spare time."

CAST OF CHARACTERS

ALONSO, King of Naples.

SEBASTIAN, Alonso's brother.

PROSPERO, the rightful Duke of Milan. In Latin, *prospero* means "I make happy, I make fortunate, I make successful."

ANTONIO, Prospero's brother, the usurping Duke of Milan.

FERDINAND, son to the King of Naples.

GONZALO, an honest old Counselor.

ADRIAN and FRANCISCO, Lords.

CALIBAN, a savage and deformed Slave.

TRINCULO, King Alonso's Jester. TRINCULO likes to drink more than enough. His name is based on the Italian *trincare*, which means "To drink."

STEPHANO, a drunken Butler.

CAPTAIN of a Ship.

BOATSWAIN, pronounced Bosun.

SAILORS.

MIRANDA, daughter to Prospero. Her name is based on the Latin *miror* and means "She who is to be admired" or "She who is to be wondered at."

ARIEL, an airy Spirit.

IRIS, goddess of the rainbow and messenger of the gods and especially messenger of Juno, Queen of the gods. Played by a spirit.

CERES, goddess of fertility and agriculture, played by Ariel.

JUNO, Queen of the gods, played by a Spirit. She is the goddess of marriage.

HARPIES, birds with the face of a woman, played by Spirits.

NYMPHS, REAPERS, DOGS: played by Spirits.

CHAPTER 1

— 1.1 —

Thunder sounded and lightning flashed as a storm struck a ship at sea.

The Captain of the ship shouted, "Boatswain!"

"Here I am, Captain. How goes it?"

"Good fellow, speak to the sailors and give them orders. All of us must get on with the work — and briskly — or else we will run aground. Hurry! Hurry!"

Both the Captain and the Boatswain had a whistle around their necks. At times the sound of wind and waves would drown out human speech, and the sailors had been trained to get their orders from the sounds of the whistles.

The Captain exited, and some sailors came on deck and started working with the ropes.

The Boatswain said to the sailors, "Good work, mates! Work with a good will, sailors! Quickly! Take in the topsail. Listen to the whistle for your orders."

He shouted at the storm, "Blow as hard as you like, as long as we are on the open sea and not close to sand reefs or rocks!"

Several passengers — members of the upper class — came on deck. They included Alonso, the King of Naples; Sebastian, Alonso's brother; Antonio, who had stolen the Dukedom of Naples from Prospero, who was his brother; Ferdinand, Alonso's son, who was a Prince; Gonzalo, an honest old counselor, and others.

King Alonso said, "Good Boatswain, take care. Where's the Captain?"

To the sailors, King Alonso said, "Be men now."

The Boatswain replied, "Please, keep below. Do not be on deck now."

Antonio, Prospero's brother, said, "Where is the Captain, Boatswain?"

The Captain's whistle could be heard, giving orders to the sailors behind the mast. The Boatswain was in charge of the sailors before the mast.

The Boatswain replied to Antonio, "Can't you hear him?"

To all the upper-class passengers, he said, "You are interfering with our work. Stay in your cabins. You are assisting the storm, not us sailors."

Gonzalo, an old counselor, said, "Good Boatswain, be calm."

"I will be calm when the sea is calm," the Boatswain said. "Get below! Alonso is the King of Naples, but what do these roaring winds and waves care for the title of King? Go to your cabins and be quiet! The only people who should be on deck now are sailors!"

Gonzalo was loyal to King Naples, right or wrong. He said, "Good Boatswain, remember whom you have on board this ship."

The Boatswain had already made it clear that he was not impressed by his passengers' titles and positions in society — certainly not when his life depended on competence in dealing with a storm at sea.

He said, "I love none of the ship's passengers more than I love myself. You are a counselor, so if your talents are useful now, put them to work. If you can command these winds and waves to be calm and if you can bring peace out of the current turmoil, we sailors will not handle any more ropes. If you can do these things, then do them. If you cannot do these things, then give thanks that you have lived so long, and go to your cabin below and prepare yourself both spiritually and physically for whatever misfortune may occur."

The Boatswain said to the sailors, "Good work, mates," and then he said to the upper-class passengers, "Get out of our way."

The Boatswain left to look after another part of the ship, and Gonzalo said, "I receive great comfort from this Boatswain. I look at him and see no indication that he will die by drowning. No, indeed, but I do see every indication that he will die by hanging. I look in his face, and I see reflected in his eyes a gallows. That is good news for us. If he does not drown today, then we probably won't drown. Stand fast, good Fate — do not let his destiny change. He who is born to be hanged shall never drown. The Fates spin the thread of life — in the Boatswain's case, that thread is a rope. Let the rope that will hang the Boatswain be our anchor chain that will keep us safe since the anchor chain we have now does little good for us. If the Boatswain was not born to be hanged, then we are in a bad way."

The upper-class passengers went below deck, and the Boatswain returned to give the sailors more orders. He wanted the correct amount of sail on the ship: enough to keep the ship moving away from the rocks, but not enough that the winds would capsize the ship and sink it. Right now, the ship was getting dangerously close to the shore of an island, and so the Boatswain wanted to lower the topmost section of the main mast to reduce the amount of weight aloft.

The Boatswain ordered, "Down with the topmast! Quickly! Lower! Lower! Lower the mainsail and keep as close to the wind as we can!"

The upper-class passengers below shouted with fright and excitement.

The Boatswain said, "Damn this howling! These passengers are louder than the roars of the winds and waves and louder than we sailors are at our work."

Sebastian, Antonio, and Gonzalo came up on deck again.

"Yet again!" the Boatswain said. "What are you doing here? Shall we give up, stop working, and drown? Do you want the ship to sink?"

Sebastian, an unpleasant man, said, "May you get cancer of the throat, you bawling, blasphemous, uncharitable dog!"

"Do some work, then!" the Boatswain replied.

Antonio, another unpleasant man, said, "Hang from the gallows, cur! Hang, you son of a whore! Hang, you insolent noisemaker! We are less afraid of being drowned than you are!"

Gonzalo said, "I still say that the Boatswain will never drown — I guarantee it — even if the ship were no stronger than a nutshell and as leaky as a menstruating woman."

The Boatswain was still trying to do his job despite the interference of the passengers: "Lay her close to the wind! Set her two courses off to sea again — let's use the main sail and the fore sail to reach the open sea again!"

Some thoroughly drenched sailors shouted, "All is lost! Pray! All is lost!"

"What! Must we die with cold mouths?" the Boatswain said. "Must we drown in the cold sea?"

Gonzalo said, "King Alonso and Prince Ferdinand are praying! Let us pray with them. They and we are in the same situation!"

Sebastian said, "I have run out of patience."

Antonio said, "We will die, and why! Because drunk sailors are cheating us of our lives! This big-mouthed Boatswain — I wish that this rascal would be hung at the low-water mark and left hanging until ten tides had washed over him, although the usual punishment for pirates is to be left hanging until only three tides wash over them."

"The Boatswain will be hanged yet," Gonzalo said, "although every drop of water swears that he will be drowned and tries its best to swallow him."

Several people cried out:

"Have mercy on us!"

"The ship is splitting in two!"

"Farewell, brother!"

"The ship is breaking up!"

Antonio said, "Let's go to King Alonso and sink with him."

Sebastian said, "Let's say goodbye to the King."

Antonio and Sebastian left, leaving Gonzalo behind, who said to himself, "I would give over a hundred miles of sea for an acre of barren ground that can grow only long heather, brown gorse, or any other kind of weed. May God's will be done! But I would prefer to die on dry ground!"

— 1.2 —

On the island, the exiled Duke of Milan, whose name was Prospero, and his daughter, whose name was Miranda, watched the storm at sea.

Miranda said, "If by your magic, my dearest father, you have put the wild waters in this uproar, calm them. The sky, it seems, would pour down stinking and burning — because struck by lightning! — black tar instead of rain, except that the sea, whose high waves climb to the face of the sky, dashes the fire out. I have suffered with those whom I saw suffer. I have seen a splendid ship that had, no doubt, some noble men in her dashed all to pieces. The cries I heard knocked against my very heart and broke it. Poor souls, they have perished. Had I been a god with enough power to control the sea, I would have sunk the sea within the earth before it would have so swallowed the good ship and the cargo of souls it carried."

"Be calm and collected," Prospero replied. "Do not be terrified any longer. Tell your heart that pities the souls on the ship that no harm has been done."

"This is a woeful day!" Miranda cried.

"No," Prospero said. "No harm has been done. I have done nothing except for you, my dear one, my daughter, who are ignorant of who you are. You know nothing of who I am or where I came from. You do not know that I am of higher rank than the Prospero you know, who is the head of a very poor dwelling and who is your father."

"I have never thought that I would learn more," Miranda said.

"It is time that I should give you more information. Help me take off my magic cloak. Thank you."

Prospero lay his magic cloak on the ground and said, "Lie there, my art."

As a magician, Prospero used a magic cloak, a magic wand, and books of magic.

Prospero and Miranda sat on the ground.

He said to his daughter, "Wipe your eyes, and be comforted. With my magic, I created this direful spectacle of the shipwreck that has aroused your virtuous compassion; however, I have used my magic in such a way that no one has been hurt. Not a single hair on anyone's head was harmed in this shipwreck that you saw, despite the cries that you heard. But sit down now because you need to learn more about your family history."

"You have often begun to tell me who I am and what our history is, but then you have stopped and have not answered any of my questions. You always told me, 'Wait! I won't tell you yet!'"

"The hour has now come for your questions to be answered," Prospero said. "This very minute you should open your ears, listen, and be attentive. Can you remember a time before we came to this island? I do not think you can because when we came here you were not fully three years old."

"Yes, sir, father, I can," Miranda said.

"What do you remember? Do you remember a house or a person? Tell me whatever you remember."

"The memory seems far distant and more like a dream than a definite recollection. But didn't I once have four or five women who took care of me?"

"Yes, you did, Miranda, and you had more women than that looking after you. But how is it that you remember this when you were so young? What else do you remember from the depths of the past? If you can remember something from the time before we came here, you may remember how we came here."

"But I do not remember that."

"Twelve years ago, Miranda, your father was the Duke of Milan and a powerful Prince."

"Sir, aren't you my father?"

"Your mother was a model of virtue, and she said that you are my daughter; as I said, your father was the Duke of Milan, and you are his only heir. You are no less noble in descent than a Princess."

"What foul play were we the victims of, that we had to leave Milan? Or was it a blessing when we left?"

"Both, my daughter," Prospero said. "By foul play, as you said, were we heaved out of Milan, but it is a blessing that we came to this island."

"My heart bleeds when I think of the trouble that I must have been to you, although I cannot even remember that time. Please tell me more."

"My brother and your uncle, whose name is Antonio — pay attention — I can't believe that a brother should be so deceitful and untrustworthy. I loved Antonio next to myself of everything in the world, and I allowed Antonio to govern Milan. At that time, Milan was the first among the city-states and I, Prospero, was the Duke of Milan — the most important Duke in Italy. I had a reputation for nobleness and excellence, and no one could rival my learning in the liberal arts, both the *trivium* — grammar, logic, and rhetoric — and the *quadrivium* — arithmetic, geometry, music, and astronomy. I studied constantly and so allowed my brother to rule Milan, delegating to him my state duties. The citizens of Milan grew accustomed to seeing my brother and seldom saw me. I also studied the art of magic — are you listening to me?"

"Very carefully, father."

"My brother learned well how to play power politics. He learned how to grant some requests and how to deny other requests. He learned whom to advance and whom to tear down because they had grown too powerful. He created allies for himself out of those who had been my allies. He also changed some people's positions and brought in new people who were loyal to him. He had the keys of office — the keys that belong to an officer — and the people at court played his tune. He became the parasitic ivy that covered the trunk and leaves of the tree that was me, and the ivy killed the tree's leaves and so killed the tree's vitality — you have stopped listening to me!"

"Good sir, I am listening, father," Miranda said.

Prospero knew that Miranda was listening, but he knew the information he was telling her was important and he wanted her to pay special attention to it.

"Please, pay attention," Prospero said. "I neglected my worldly duties and dedicated myself to seclusion and the bettering of my mind with knowledge that was of greater value than most people would value it. My trust in my brother was without limit, without bound. A good parent often has a bad child. My trust in my brother was like that of a good parent, but it gave birth in my brother to evil desires — because I neglected my Duke's duties and remained secluded in order to study, the evil in my brother's nature awoke. He had the power of the Duke of Milan, and he had the income of the Duke of Milan — along with whatever other income his power allowed him to extort. He became used to the power and the income, and he began to think that he — not I — was the real Duke of Milan. He told himself this lie so often that he believed it and so made

his memory commit a sin against truth. His ambition grew —
are you still listening, daughter?"

"Your tale, sir, would cure deafness," Miranda said.

Prospero thought, *The acquisition of knowledge is good, but
so is doing your duty. I neglected to do my duty as Duke of Milan.
It would have been better for everyone, including my brother, if I
had done my political duty instead of studying magic. In this case,
the study I undertook should have been whatever study would
help me to become a better political ruler.*

"My brother wanted nothing to separate the real Duke of
Milan and the person who performed the role of the Duke of
Milan, and so he decided that he needed to be the real Duke of
Milan. He thought that for me, poor me, my library was a large
enough Dukedom. He thought that I was no longer competent
to govern worldly affairs. Therefore, he conspired — he was so
thirsty for power — with the King of Naples. He agreed to give
the King of Naples annual tribute, do him homage, subject his
coronet to the King of Naples' crown, and make the Dukedom
of Milan — which had been previously unbowed — bend in
homage to the Kingdom of Naples."

"Oh, in the name of Heaven!" Miranda said.

"Note the agreement that he made with the King of Naples
and the outcome that resulted, and then tell me whether he
acted like a brother," Prospero said.

"I would sin if I were to think anything but that my
grandmother was noble," Miranda said. "Good wombs have
borne bad sons."

"This is the agreement that my brother made with the King
of Naples, who was always an enemy to me," Prospero said.
"In return for homage and I know not how much tribute, the

King of Naples agreed that he would immediately drive out of Milan my allies and me and allow Antonio, my brother, to be the Duke of Milan. After they made the agreement, the King of Naples raised a treacherous army, and Antonio at midnight opened the gates of Milan, and in the dead of darkness the agents appointed for the purpose hurried away from Milan me and you, my crying daughter."

"I pity you because of what you went through," Miranda said. "I don't remember crying then, so I will cry now. This is a story that wrings tears from my eyes."

"Hear a little more about the past, and then I will talk about the present business that is now at hand. Unless you understand what has happened in the past, you will not understand what is happening now."

"Why didn't our enemies kill us the night they took us from Milan?"

"You ask a good question, daughter," Prospero said. "My story does need to answer that question. Dear, they dared not kill us outright because my people loved me dearly. They could not kill us openly and bloodily, but instead they had to hide what they wanted to do. Briefly, they hurried us aboard a boat that carried us to the sea. There they prepared a rotten carcass of a boat; it was not fitted out for a sea voyage. It had no ropes, no sails, and no masts. Even the rats had instinctively deserted this rotten skeleton of a boat. Our enemies put us in the boat and left us to cry to the sea that roared at us and to sigh to the winds that pityingly sighed back at us; unfortunately, this added to our discomfort."

"I must have been a burden to you," Miranda said.

"You were no burden," Prospero replied. "You were an angel who saved me. You smiled — you must have been infused with fortitude from Heaven. After I had cried and added my salt tears to the salt water of the sea and after I had groaned because of our desperate situation, I saw you smile and the courage to endure was born in me and so I was able to bear up against distress and withstand everything that ensued."

"How did we come ashore?"

"We were assisted by divine Providence," Prospero said. "A noble Neapolitan, Gonzalo, was charitable. He gave us food and fresh water, as well as rich clothing, linens, household equipment, and necessities, which have ever since been very useful to us. He knew that I loved my books, and his noble character led him to supply me with volumes from my own library — books of magic that I prize above my Dukedom."

"I wish that I could see that kind man someday!"

"Now I will stand up. Stay seated, daughter," Prospero said. He put on his magic cloak and said, "Listen to the last of our sorrows at sea. Here at this island we arrived; and here have I, your schoolmaster, educated you better than other royal children who have more time to waste and tutors who do not take the pains that I do."

Prospero thought, *Females should be educated well, just like males; this world needs good brains. If we neglect human female brains, we are neglecting half of the human brains in this world.*

"May God bless you for my education! And now, please, sir, father, for I still want to know, what is your reason for raising this tempest at sea?"

"You should know this. The goddess Fortune, bountiful Fortune, who was once my enemy, now favors me. By a strange accident, Fortune has brought my enemies to this shore. Because of my studies of magic, I know that my future depends on what I do now. I can reach my zenith — my highest point — if I seize the opportunity promised to me by a most auspicious star. But if I ignore this opportunity, my fortunes will forever after droop. Now ask no more questions."

Prospero thought, *The same knowledge can result in good or ill. My study of magic helped me lose my Dukedom because I neglected my political duties; however, my study of magic can help me to regain my Dukedom. If I do regain my Dukedom, I will need to concentrate on doing my political duties, not on studying magic.*

With a wave of his hand, Prospero cast a spell to make Miranda sleep. He said to her, "You are growing sleepy. It is a good drowsiness; give in to it. I know that you cannot choose to resist it."

Miranda slept.

Prospero then said into the air, "Come away from wherever you are, servant, come away. I am ready to talk to you now. Approach, my Ariel, and come to me."

A shape-shifting immortal spirit of the air, Ariel could appear as either male or female, but was neither.

In the form of a young man, Ariel flew to Prospero and said, "Greetings, great master! Grave sir, greetings! I come to do your will, whatever it is: to fly, to swim, to dive into the fire, or to ride on the curled clouds. Ariel and all of Ariel's colleagues will do whatever you wish."

"Have you, spirit, performed in every detail what I told you to do in creating the tempest?"

"Yes, every detail," Ariel answered. "I boarded the King of Naples' ship. In the prow, amidships, on the poop deck, in every cabin, and here and there and now and again I flamed like St. Elmo's fire and caused amazement. Sometimes I would divide myself and burn in many places. I would burn as separate flames on the topmast, the yardarms, and the bowsprit, and then meet and join together as one single flame. The Roman god Jove's lightning bolts, which are the precursors of dreadful thunderclaps, were not more instantaneous and quicker than sight than I was. The fire and the deafening cracks of burning sulphur seemed to besiege the most mighty Neptune, god of the sea, and make his bold waves tremble. Indeed, his dread trident shook."

"My splendid spirit!" Prospero said. "Was anyone so firm, so level-headed, that this disturbed confusion did not infect his reason and make him irrational?"

"Every soul felt a fever such as madmen suffer from," Ariel answered. "Every soul did deeds of desperation. Everyone except for the mariners plunged into the foaming brine and abandoned the ship that was then all afire with me. The King's son, Ferdinand, whose hair was standing on end and looked like reeds, not hair, was the first man who leaped into the sea, crying as he jumped, 'Hell is empty, and all the devils are here.'"

"Why, that's my spirit!" Prospero said. "And did this happen near shore?"

"It happened close to shore, master," Ariel replied.

"Ariel, are the inhabitants of the ship safe?"

"Not a hair was harmed. Their wet garments trapped air and kept them above the water; these garments bear not a single blemish and are fresher than before their wearers jumped into the sea. As you ordered me, I have most of them dispersed in groups about the island. Only the King's son, Ferdinand, is alone. I landed him by himself, and I left him cooling the air with sighs in an odd corner of the island. He is sitting with his arms crossed together in a sad knot."

"Tell me what has happened to the ship's sailors and to the rest of the fleet that was sailing with the King of Naples."

"The King's ship is safely in the harbor," Ariel replied. "It is in the deep bay, where once you called me up at midnight to fetch dew from the storm-vexed Bermuda islands to use in your magic. In that deep bay, the ship is hidden. The sailors are all stowed below deck. I left them asleep, exhausted from their labor and charmed by my sleeping spell. As for the rest of the fleet that I dispersed with the tempest, they all have met together again and are sailing upon the Mediterranean sea, bound sadly home for Naples, believing that they saw the King's ship wrecked and the King himself drowned."

"Ariel, you have exactly performed what I ordered you to do, but more work remains to be done. What time is it?"

"It is past noon."

"It is at least two o'clock," Prospero said. "The time between six o'clock and now must by us both be spent most preciously and wisely."

"Is there more toil?" Ariel asked. "Since you give me hard tasks to do, let me remind you what you have promised to me, a thing that you have not yet done."

Prospero was not happy. Ariel had just promised a willingness to do many tasks — "I come to do your will, whatever it is: to fly, to swim, to dive into the fire, or to ride on the curled clouds. Ariel and all of his colleagues will do whatever you wish" — and now Ariel seemed not so willing to work for Prospero. Important events were at hand, and Prospero needed Ariel's help. Still, he pretended to be angrier than he really was — he had good news for Ariel, and pretended anger now would make the later good news a splendid surprise.

"What is this?" Prospero asked. "Are you in a bad mood? What is it that you can demand?"

"My liberty."

"Before the time of your servitude is over? I want to hear no more about this!"

"Please, remember that I have done worthy service for you. I have told you no lies, made no mistakes, served you without grudge or grumblings. You promised that if I served you well that you would reduce the period of my servitude by one full year."

Prospero replied, "Have you forgotten from what torment I freed you?"

"No."

"Yes, you have forgotten, and now you think it is too hard a task for you to do my will and tread the ooze of the bottom of the salty sea, to ride upon the sharp wind of the north, and to do my bidding underground when the earth is hardened with frost."

"I do not, sir."

"You lie, rebellious thing!" Prospero said. "Have you forgotten the foul witch Sycorax, who with age and malice and evil grew into the shape of a hoop? She was so stooped over that her chin met her knees. Have you forgotten her?"

"No, sir."

"You have forgotten her. Where was she born? Speak; tell me."

"Sir, in Algiers."

"So you remember that, but because you so often forget the past, I must recount once each month in what a bad situation you have been. This damned witch Sycorax, because of many and various mischiefs and terrible sorceries that human ears ought not to hear, was banished from Algiers, as you know. Because of one thing, the people of Algiers would not take her life. Isn't this true?"

"Yes, sir."

"This hag with a bluish shadow on her eyelids — a sign of pregnancy — was brought here heavy with child and here the sailors left her. You, my slave, as you call yourself, were then her servant. Because you were a spirit too delicate to obey her earthy and abhorred commands, you refused to carry out the orders she most wanted you to carry out."

Prospero thought, *You, Ariel, have never refused to carry out my orders. This is evidence that my orders are not evil.*

Prospero added, "In response, she punished you. With the help of her more potent ministers — the agents of Satan — she confined you within a cloven pine, where you painfully remained a dozen years, within which time she died and left you there. You groaned with pain as often as the paddles of a millhouse wheel strike the water. During that time, this island had no being who bore a human shape, except for the son that she littered here — a freckled whelp given birth to by a hag."

"Yes, Caliban, her son."

Prospero, resenting the interruption, said, "You dunce! Of course, I mean Caliban! Caliban now works as my servant. You best know in what torment I found you. Your groans made wolves howl and penetrated the breasts of always-angry bears. The torment you endured was suitable for one of the damned, and Sycorax, being dead, could never free you from the cloven pine, but when I arrived on this island and heard your groans, I used my magic art and made the pine open and release you."

"Thank you, master."

"If you continue to complain, I will rend an oak open and plant you in its knotty entrails until you have howled away twelve winters."

"I beg your pardon, master," Ariel said. "I will obey your commands and perform my tasks without complaining."

Prosper smiled at Ariel, and said, "Do that, and after two days I will set you free."

The surprise good news had the effect on Ariel that Prospero had hoped for.

"You are a noble master!" Ariel happily exclaimed. "What shall I do? Tell me what you want me to do."

"Assume the shape of a sea-nymph — a female water spirit," Prospero ordered. "Be invisible to everyone except you and me. Go now, transform, and return. I know that shape-shifting takes effort and time — do it properly."

Ariel exited, and Prospero thought, *Ariel will be invisible to everyone except himself and me. Why should Ariel assume the form of a sea-nymph — a beautiful goddess of the sea? I haven't seen a woman in 12 years! Why shouldn't I have something pretty to look at?*

Prospero said to Miranda, "Awake, dear heart, awake! You have slept well. Wake up!"

Miranda said, "The strangeness of your story made me sleepy."

"Shake it off," Prospero said. "Come on. We'll visit Caliban, my slave, who never gives us a kind answer."

"He is a villain, sir, whom I do not like to look at."

"True, but we cannot do without him. He makes our fire, fetches in our wood, and performs other services that benefit us."

They arrived quickly at Caliban's cave, and Prospero called, "Slave! Caliban! Being of earth! Answer me."

From within the cave, Caliban replied, "You have enough firewood to do you for a while."

"Come forth from your cave, I say!" Prospero said. "There is other work for you to do. Come, you tortoise! Hurry!"

Having assumed the shape of a water-nymph, Ariel flew to Prospero, who said, "You are a fine apparition! My elegant Ariel, listen to me. I have work for you to do."

Miranda was used to seeing spirits on the island, although now Ariel was invisible.

Prospero whispered in Ariel's ear, and Ariel said, "My Lord, it shall be done."

Ariel exited, and Prospero shouted to Caliban, "You poisonous slave, begotten by the devil himself upon your wicked dam, Sycorax, come here!"

Caliban came out of his cave and said, "May dew as wicked as ever my mother brushed with an ill-omened raven's feather from an unwholesome marsh drop on you both! May an unwholesome southwest wind blow on you and blister you all over!"

"Because of your ill words, tonight you shall have cramps — side-stitches that will stop your breath," Prospero said. "Goblins in the form of hedgehogs shall, during nighttime, when they do their evil work, torment you. You shall be tormented as many times as honeycombs have cells. Each torment will sting you more painfully than each sting of the bees that made the honeycombs."

"I must eat my dinner," Caliban said. "This island, which you have taken from me, is mine. I inherited this island from Sycorax, my mother. When you first came here, you patted me and made much of me. You would give me water with berries in it, and you would teach me the name of the bigger light — the Sun — and the lesser light — the Moon — that burn by day and night. Then I loved you and showed you all the features of the island: the fresh springs and the brine-pits as well as the barren places and the fertile places. Cursed be Caliban because Caliban did so! May all the evil spells of Sycorax, as well as toads, beetles, and bats, fall on you! I am all the subjects whom you have: just one. And I used to be my own King. But now here you pen me up like a pig in this cave in this hard rock, and you keep me from visiting the rest of the island."

"You are a constantly lying slave, whom stripes made by whips may move, not kindness!" Prospero replied. "I have treated you, filth as I now know you are, with humane care, and I lodged you in my own dwelling until you tried to rape my daughter, Miranda."

"Ha!" Caliban laughed. "I wish that I had raped her! You stopped me, or else I would have populated this island with many Calibans."

"Abhorred slave," Miranda replied, "you are incapable of doing any good and you are capable of doing any evil. I pitied you, took pains to teach you to speak, and taught you something new each hour. Back when you did not — savage as you were — know your own meaning, but would instead gabble like a most brutish thing, I endowed you with the power of speech so that you could make your meaning known. But your blood is bad, and although you did learn, good people cannot bear to be around you — a would-be rapist! Therefore, you have deserved to be confined in this cave. In fact, you deserve to be punished more harshly than merely to be placed in a prison."

Caliban replied, "You taught me language; and my profit from learning it is that I know how to curse. May the red plague destroy you because you taught me your language!"

Prospero thought, *Education is important, but more important than education is having a good character — one that wishes to do good instead of evil. Miranda benefited greatly from education because she has a good character.*

Prospero said to Caliban, "Hag-seed, go now! Fetch firewood, and be quick to obey — if you know what is good for you — when I have other tasks for you. Do you dare resist me, malicious thing? If you neglect or do unwillingly what I command you to do, I will torment you with cramps and with aches in the bones like those suffered by the old. I will make you roar so loudly that beasts shall tremble at your din."

"Please, no," Caliban said.

He thought, *I must obey Prospero; his art is of such power that it could control my dam's god, Setebos, and make a servant out of him.*

"Slave, leave us now and gather firewood!" Prospero said. Caliban exited.

In the form of a sea-nymph, Ariel now came toward Prospero and Miranda. Ariel was performing the task that Prospero had earlier given to the spirit: to lead Ferdinand, the son of the King of Naples, to Prospero and Miranda. Ariel was invisible to Ferdinand as Ariel sang and played music.

Ariel sang this song:

"Come unto these yellow sands,

"And then take hands:

"When you have curtsied and kissed

"The wild waves into silence,

"Dance daintily here and there;

"And, sweet spirits, the bass undersong bear.

"Hark, hark!"

This was followed by the spirits barking like dogs here and there.

Ariel sang, *"The watch-dogs bark!"*

This was again followed by the spirits barking like dogs here and there.

Ariel sang again:

"Hark, hark! I hear

"The song of strutting chanticleer

"Cry, Cock-a-doodle-do."

Spirits sang — not all at the same time — the sound of a crowing rooster.

Ferdinand heard the song and the music, but he could not see Ariel. He said, "Where is this music coming from? The air or the earth? I can no longer hear it. No doubt the music serves some god on the island. As I was sitting on a bank by the seashore, mourning again the shipwreck and the death of my father, Alonso, the King of Naples, I heard this music creep by me upon the water. With its sweet air, the music calmed both the water's fury and my suffering. I followed the music, or rather it drew me here. But the music has gone. No, it begins again."

Ariel sang this song:
"*Full five fathoms deep your father lies;*
"*Of his bones is coral made;*
"*Those are pearls that were his eyes:*
"*All of him that does fade*
"*Will suffer a sea-change*
"*Into something rich and strange.*
"*Sea-nymphs hourly ring his knell.*"

This was followed by the spirits ding-donging — not all at the same time — like bells.

Ariel sang, "*Listen! Now I hear them — ding-dong, bell.*"

Ferdinand said, "This song commemorates my drowned father. This is no mortal business; this is no sound that the earth owns. I hear it coming now from above me."

Prospero said to his daughter, Miranda, "Raise the fringed curtains — the eyelids — of your eyes and tell me what you see over there."

Miranda replied, "What is it? A spirit? Lord, how it looks around! Believe me, sir, the spirit has assumed a handsome form. But it is a spirit."

"No, lass," Prospero said. "It eats and sleeps and has such senses as we have. This fine fellow whom you see was in the ship that wrecked, and, if he were not somewhat stained with grief — a spoiler of good looks — you might call him a good-looking man. He has been separated from his fellow travelers and is looking around for them."

"I might call him divine, for I have never seen anything natural that looked so noble."

Prospero whispered to Ariel, "My plan is working. Miranda is falling in love with Ferdinand. Ariel, fine spirit! I'll free you within two days for helping me accomplish this."

Ferdinand saw Miranda and said, "This must be the goddess of this island. Music plays for her!"

He said to Miranda, "Grant my request and tell me whether you dwell on this island. Give me good advice about how I may properly behave here. My most important request, which I make last, is — you are a wonder! — tell me whether you are human and whether you are married?"

"I am no wonder, sir," Miranda said, "but I am certainly an unmarried and human maiden."

"You speak my language!" Ferdinand said. "Heavens! I am the highest in rank of them who speak this language — if I were where this language is spoken."

Prospero wanted Miranda and Ferdinand to fall in love, but part of his plan was to make Ferdinand's life difficult for a while. He said to Ferdinand, "How can you be the highest in rank? What would you be if the King of Naples heard you?"

"I would still be a solitary man — exactly as I am now — who wonders at hearing you speak of Naples," Ferdinand replied. "The King of Naples does hear me, and because he does hear me, I grieve. I myself am the King of Naples. My eyes have never stopped crying since I saw my father the King shipwrecked and drowned."

"How awful!" Miranda said.

"Yes, it is," Ferdinand said. "I saw my father and all his Lords die. Two of those who died were the Duke of Milan and his splendid son."

Prospero whispered to Ariel, "The rightful Duke of Milan — me — and his more splendid daughter could challenge that assertion if now was the right time to do so. Soon enough, Ferdinand will find out that his father and everyone else on the ship survived and are in good health. But right now something important is happening. Ferdinand and Miranda have exchanged glances and fallen in love at first sight. Exquisite Ariel, I'll set you free because of this."

Prospero said to Ferdinand, "A word, good sir; I fear you have done yourself some wrong. You have said something about yourself that is not true."

Miranda thought, *Why is my father speaking so rudely? This is the third man whom I have ever seen; the other two are my father and Caliban. This is the first man whom I ever fell in love with and sighed for. May pity for me move my father to like this man.*

Ferdinand said to Miranda, "If you are an unmarried virgin who is not in love with someone else, I will make you the Queen of Naples."

"Just a minute, sir!" Prospero said. "I have more to say to you."

Prospero thought, *They are both in each other's power —they are in love — but I must interrupt this too-swift falling in love. A prize too easily won is not properly valued.*

Prospero said to Ferdinand, "One thing more. You must hear what I have to say to you. You have usurped a title that does not belong to you — you are not the King of Naples.

Indeed, you came to this island to be a spy and steal it away from me, its rightful ruler."

"No, I swear that that is not true!" Ferdinand said.

Miranda said to Ferdinand, "A man as handsome as you is a temple in which nothing evil can dwell. If Satan were as handsome as you, goodness would strive to dwell within him. According to Renaissance Neo-Platonic philosophers, beauty of spirit and beauty of form are inseparable."

"Follow me," Prospero said to Ferdinand.

To Miranda, Prospero said, "Don't try to defend him — he's a traitor."

He said to Ferdinand, "Come with me. I will chain your neck and feet together. You will drink seawater, and your food will be inedible fresh-brook mussels, withered roots, and the caps of acorns. Follow me."

"No," Ferdinand said. "I will resist such treatment until my enemy has more power and strength than I do."

He drew his sword, but Prospero used his magic to paralyze him and keep him from moving.

Miranda said, "Dear father, don't judge him so hastily. He is a gentleman of noble birth whom you ought not to fear."

"What?" Prospero said. "Will my foot — something that is beneath me — teach my head? Should I take advice from my own very young daughter?"

He said to Ferdinand, "Put your sword away, traitor. You make a show of courage, but you dare not strike me because you have a guilty conscience. Come out of your fencing posture because I can use my wand to easily disarm you and make your weapon drop."

Ferdinand dropped his sword.

Miranda grabbed her father's cloak and said, "Please, father, I beg you not to harm him."

"Get away from me, Miranda! Let go of my clothing!"

"Sir, have pity on him. I guarantee that he will not cause trouble."

"Silence! One word more shall make me reprimand you and maybe even hate you. What! You want to defend an imposter! Be quiet! Do you think that no more men like him exist because you have seen only him and Caliban? Foolish girl! Compared to most men, this man is a Caliban. Compared to this man, most men are angels."

"My love, then, is very humble," Miranda said. "I have no desire to see a better-looking man."

Prospero said to Ferdinand, "Come on; obey me. Your muscles are once more in their infancy and have no strength. You can move only weakly."

"You speak truly," Ferdinand replied. "My strength is gone, and it is as if I were attempting to move in a dream. Still, the death of my father, this weakness that I feel, the shipwreck of all my friends, and the threats of this magician who has taken me prisoner would all be light burdens to me if only once a day I could see this maiden from my prison. Let free men make use of all the rest of the Earth. As long as I can see this maiden once a day, a prison is room enough for me."

Prospero thought, *He is definitely in love with my daughter. My plan is working.*

To Ferdinand, he said, "Come with me."

To Ariel, he said, "You have done well, fine spirit!"

To Ferdinand, he said, "Follow me."

To Ariel, he said, "Listen as I tell you something else I need you to do for me."

Prospero spoke quietly to Ariel while Miranda spoke to Ferdinand.

Miranda said to Ferdinand, "Don't worry. My father has a better nature, sir, than he appears to have by his speech now. What he said is uncharacteristic of him."

Prospero said to Ariel, "You shall be as free as the mountain winds, but first do exactly what I tell you to do."

"I will obey every syllable," Ariel replied.

Prospero said to Ferdinand, "Come now and follow me."

He said to Miranda, "Don't try to defend him."

CHAPTER 2

— 2.1 —

In another part of the island, several members of the upper class who had escaped from the shipwreck were talking together. They included Alonso, the King of Naples; Sebastian, Alonso's brother; Antonio, Prospero's brother and the usurping Duke of Milan; Gonzalo, an honest old counselor; and two Lords named Adrian and Francisco. Sebastian and Antonio stood a short distance away from the others.

Gonzalo said to Alonso, King of Naples, "Please, sir, be happy. You have cause, as do we all, for being joyful. Our lives are far more important than the material possessions we have lost. What we have suffered in this shipwreck, others have often suffered. Everyday some sailor's wife, the captains of merchant ships and the merchants themselves suffer because of shipwrecks. We ourselves have benefited from a miracle that preserved our lives, which few people out of millions have experienced. Good sir, wisely weigh our sorrows against our blessings."

King Alonso was mourning because he thought that his son, Ferdinand, had died during the shipwreck. He said, "Please, be quiet. Let your mouth be at peace."

Sebastian whispered to Antonio, "Alonso receives comforting words the way that he would receive a bowl of cold porridge that had been made with peas."

Antonio whispered back, "Gonzalo is like a visitor determined to help a sick person. He will not easily give up trying to comfort King Alonso."

Sebastian whispered, "Look, Gonzalo is winding up the watch of his wit; soon it will strike."

Gonzalo began to speak to King Alonso: "Sir —"

Sebastian whispered, "It has struck once. Let's keep count of how many times his wit will strike."

Gonzalo said, "When we entertain — that is, admit and accept — every grief that comes our way, then there comes to the entertainer —"

Sebastian said, "A dollar."

He had spoken loudly enough for Gonzalo to overhear him.

Gonzalo was quick witted and punned, "Dolor — that is, sorrow — comes to him, indeed. You, Sebastian, have spoken truer than you supposed."

"You have taken it wiselier than I meant you should," Sebastian said.

Gonzalo continued, "Therefore, my Lord —"

Antonio and Sebastian continued to speak to each other. They were annoyed and often did not lower their voices as much as they should have.

Antonio said, "Gosh, what a spendthrift is he of his tongue! He does not save his words!"

King Alonso said to Gonzalo, "Please, stop talking to me."

Gonzalo replied, "Well, I have finished." He hesitated and then added, "But yet —"

Sebastian finished the sentence: "— he will be talking."

Antonio whispered, "Let's make a bet. Who — Gonzalo or Adrian — will be the first one to talk? Who will be the first one to crow?"

Sebastian whispered, "I bet on the old cock — Gonzalo."

Antonio whispered, "I bet on the young cockerel — Adrian."

Sebastian whispered, "Agreed. What are we betting for?"

"A good laugh. He who wins, laughs."

"Agreed."

Adrian said, "Although this island seems to be deserted —"

Antonio laughed.

Sebastian whispered, "You won — and you have been paid with a good laugh."

Adrian continued, "— uninhabitable, and almost inaccessible —"

Sebastian whispered, "His next word will be 'yet.'"

Adrian said, "— yet —"

Antonio whispered, "He was bound to say that."

Adrian said, "— it has a subtle and tender and delicate and temperate climate."

Antonio said, "I once knew a woman named Temperance — she was a wench who was not temperate when it came to sexual pleasure."

Sebastian agreed, "True, she knew subtle and tender and delicate bedroom tricks. Adrian speaks more interestingly than he knows."

Adrian said, "The air breathes and blows upon us here most sweetly."

Sebastian said, "In my opinion, the blow comes from rotten lungs."

Antonio added, "The breath seems to be perfumed by a swamp."

Gonzalo said, "On this island is everything advantageous to life."

Antonio said, "True, except the means to live."

"Of that there's none, or little," Sebastian said.

"How lush and healthy the grass looks!" Gonzalo said, "How green the grass is!"

"The ground indeed is reddish-brown," Antonio said.

"With a touch of green in it," Sebastian said.

"Gonzalo does not miss seeing much," Antonio said.

"No, he doesn't," Sebastian said, "but he entirely misinterprets what he sees."

Gonzalo said, "But the rarity of it is — which is indeed almost beyond credit —"

"— as many vouched-for rarities are," Sebastian said.

"— that our garments, being, as they were, drenched in the sea, are nonetheless still fresh and appear lustrous. They seem to be newly dyed rather than stained with seawater," Gonzalo said.

Antonio said to Sebastian, "If one of Gonzalo's pockets could speak, wouldn't it say he lies?"

"Yes," Sebastian said. "If his pocket did not say he lies, his pocket would pocket the evidence and ignore the lie."

Gonzalo said, "I think that our garments are now as fresh as when we put them on first in Africa, at the marriage of our King of Naples' fair daughter, Clarabel, to the King of Tunis."

Sebastian said sarcastically, "It was a sweet marriage, and we are prospering well in our return."

Adrian said, "Tunis was never graced before with such a paragon as its Queen."

Gonzalo said, "Not since the widow Dido's time."

Antonio said, "Widow! Please! Yes, Dido was a widow who fled the city of Tyre after her brother murdered her husband, but Gonzalo is using the word 'widow' to avoid talking about the illicit affair that Dido had with Aeneas after she founded Carthage. No one thinks of Dido as a widow! We think of her as a woman who was abandoned by her lover!"

Sebastian said, "What if he had said 'widower Aeneas,' too? Good Lord, how you would take it! Aeneas was a widower because his wife died during the fall of Troy, but no one thinks of him as a widower. We think of him as a man who abandoned his Carthaginian lover so that he could find a new wife in Italy."

Adrian said, "'Widow Dido' — of Tunis, you said? You make me wonder about that. Dido was of Carthage, not of Tunis."

"This Tunis, sir, was Carthage in ancient times," Gonzalo said.

"Was it Carthage?" Adrian asked.

"I assure you that yes, it was Carthage," Gonzalo said.

Sebastian said, "Actually, Tunis and Carthage were two separate cities that were near each other. After Carthage fell to the Romans, Tunis became the dominant city in the area. Gonzalo has made quite a mistake. According to mythology, the miraculous harp of Amphion raised the walls of the Greek city Thebes. Gonzalo's mistaken words have raised not just the walls of a city — where it does not belong — but all the houses of the city, too."

"What impossible matter will he easily accomplish next?" Antonio asked.

Sebastian replied, "I think he will carry this island home in his pocket and give it to his son and say that it is an apple."

"And, after sowing its seeds in the sea, he will bring forth more islands," Antonio said.

"Yes, indeed," Gonzalo said, referring to his — incorrect — assertion that Tunis was Carthage in ancient times.

"Yes, indeed, he will," Antonio said, referring to his and Sebastian's joke that Gonzalo would carry the island home in his pocket, say that the island was an apple, and use its seeds to create more islands.

Gonzalo still wanted to cheer up King Alonso, to whom he said, "Sir, we were saying that our garments seem now to be as fresh as when we were at Tunis at the marriage of your daughter, who is now Queen."

Antonio said, "She is the most remarkable and most beautiful Queen who ever came there."

"Except, of course, for widow Dido," Sebastian said.

"Yes, widow Dido," Antonio said. "Of course, widow Dido."

Gonzalo asked King Alonso, "Is not, sir, my jacket as fresh as the first day I wore it? I mean, in a way."

"That word 'way' was well chosen," Antonio said. "He weighed well his choice of words."

Gonzalo said, "I wore it at your daughter's wedding."

King Alonso was much annoyed and said to Gonzalo, "You cram these words into my ears against my will. I have no stomach for your words. I wish that I had never married my daughter to a King in North Africa! Because I did that, I have lost my son, who has drowned. He is lost to me, and I believe that my daughter is lost to me as well. She is so far from Italy now that I shall never see her again. As for my son — who would have had power in both Naples and Milan — what strange fish are eating my son's flesh?"

Gonzalo said, "Sir, your son may still be alive. I saw him beat the waves under him and ride upon their backs; he treaded the water, whose hatred he flung aside, and breasted the most swollen waves that came to him. Your son seemed to ride the waves. His bold head he kept above the contentious waves, and with his strong arms he oared himself with lusty strokes to the shore. The bottom of the shore's bank had been worn away by waves so that the bank seemed to lean over to welcome him. I do not doubt that your son reached land safely."

"No, no, he's dead and gone," King Alonso said.

Sebastian and Antonio resented the situation they were in; that is one reason why they had been so cynical and mocking in their conversation. Now Sebastian's resentment came pouring forth.

Sebastian, who was King Alonso's brother, said to him, "Sir, you may thank yourself for this great loss of your son. You would not bless our Europe with your daughter by marrying her to a European King; instead, you preferred to lose your daughter by marrying her to an African King. At best, she has been banished from your eyes — you will never see her again. Your eyes have reason to grieve both for your daughter and for your son."

"Please — shut up," King Alonso said.

Sebastian continued, "All of us kneeled before you and begged you to marry your daughter to a European King. Your daughter — fair soul — herself wavered over what to do: Should she rebel against a marriage she loathed or be an obedient daughter and marry the African King you chose for her? We have lost your son, I am afraid, forever. Because of this marriage you arranged, Milan and Naples have more widows in them than we will bring men — the survivors — home to comfort them. Yes, we will return — eventually — to Milan and Naples, but the rest of your fleet has been lost and the men in those ships drowned. The blame for all of this loss of life is yours."

"Also mine is the dearest of the loss of life — the loss of life of my son," King Alonso replied.

Gonzalo said, "Lord Sebastian, the truth you speak lacks gentleness. This is not the right time to speak these words. You are rubbing the sore and making it hurt when you ought to be bringing bandages and stopping the pain."

"Very well," Sebastian said. "I will stop."

Antonio said, "Gonzalo speaks like a doctor."

Gonzalo said, "King Alonso, when you are in a bad mood, it affects all of us. Foul weather is inside us all, good sir, when you are cloudy."

"Foul weather?" Sebastian said.

"Very foul," Antonio said.

Gonzalo said, "If I were able to colonize this island, King Alonso —"

"He would sow it with the seeds of nettles," Antonio said.

"Or other kinds of weeds," Sebastian said.

Gonzalo finished, "— and were the King of this island, do you know what would I do?"

"Stay sober because of lack of wine," Sebastian said.

Gonzalo said, "In my perfect colony, I would do the opposite of what is expected in all things. I would have no business trade, no judges, no education, no riches, no poverty, no servants, no contracts, no inheritances, no boundaries or division of land, no tillage, no vineyards, no use of metal, no corn, no wine, no oil, and no work. All men would be idle, and all women, too. The women would be innocent and pure. I would have no Kings —"

Sebastian said, "Yet he would be King of the island."

Antonio added, "What he said at the beginning, he has forgotten at the end."

Gonzalo continued, "Nature would produce all things for the use of everybody without human sweat or work. I would not have treason, crime, swords, pikes, knives, guns, or any kind of instrument of war. Nature would bring forth, by itself with no help from humans, everything in abundance to feed my innocent people."

Sebastian asked, "Would there be no marriage among his subjects?"

"Idleness is the nurse of lechery," Antonio said. "All of his subjects would be idle, so they would all be whores and knaves. Besides, marriage is a contract, and he would have no contracts on his island."

Gonzalo summarized his description of his perfect commonwealth, "I would with such perfection govern, sir, that life in my commonwealth would excel life during the Golden Age."

Sebastian exclaimed, "God save his majesty!"

"Long live Gonzalo!" Antonio exclaimed.

Gonzalo said, "And —" But becoming aware that King Alonso was not paying attention, he asked, "Are you listening to me, sir?"

"Please, talk to me no longer," King Alonso said. "You are talking nonsense."

"Your Highness is correct," Gonzalo said. "I have been saying these things to amuse these gentlemen, Antonio and Sebastian, who are of such sensitive and nimble lungs that they always are accustomed to laugh at nothing."

Antonio said, "It was you we laughed at."

Gonzalo replied, "I am a man who in this kind of merry fooling is nothing to you; therefore, you may continue as you are accustomed to act and laugh at nothing still."

"What a blow did Gonzalo give!" Antonio said.

"Yes — if it had not fallen flat," Sebastian said. "It is like a blow given with a flat side of a metal sword. It is a supposedly cutting remark that does not cut."

"You are gentlemen of brave mettle," Gonzalo said. "You would steal the Moon except that she outsmarts you by constantly changing and making you insane."

Ariel, who was invisible, now walked up to the men and played solemn music.

"We would steal the Moon," Sebastian said, "and use its light as a lantern to hunt birds at night."

Antonio said, "Gonzalo, don't be angry."

"No, I will not, I promise you," Gonzalo, who was angry, said. "I will not risk my good reputation for discretion for so weak a reason. Will you laugh me to sleep? I am getting very drowsy."

Antonio replied, "Go to sleep, and listen to our laughter."

Ariel's task was to use music to make some of the men fall asleep.

Everyone except King Alonso, Antonio, and Sebastian fell asleep.

King Alonso said, "I am surprised that they all fell asleep so quickly! I wish that I could go to sleep and stop thinking my sad thoughts. I do feel drowsy."

Sebastian said, "Please, sir, do not fight against sleep, which seldom visits sorrowing people. When sleep comes to a mourning person, it comforts that person."

Antonio said, "We two, my Lord, will guard you while you sleep. We will make sure that you are safe."

"Thank you," King Alonso said. "I am amazingly sleepy."

King Alonso slept, and Ariel stopped playing music and left.

The only two men left awake were Sebastian, who was King Alonso's brother, and Antonio, who had betrayed Prospero, who was his brother, and had become Duke of Milan.

"What a strange drowsiness possesses them!" Sebastian marveled.

"The climate makes them sleep," Antonio said.

"If that is true, then why aren't we sleepy? I am not at all sleepy."

"Neither am I," Antonio said. "I am wide awake. They fell asleep all at the same time, as if they — or someone — had planned it. They fell to the ground as if they had been hit by lightning. What might, worthy Sebastian ... oh, what might come from this ... I will say no more ... and yet I think I see in your face that which you should be ... opportunity is knocking for you, and my strong imagination sees a crown dropping upon your head."

Antonio had gotten an important title through treachery, so why shouldn't Sebastian?

"Are you awake or dreaming?" Sebastian asked.

"Can't you hear me speak?"

"I can," Sebastian replied, "but you certainly speak a sleepy, dreamlike language, and you are speaking as if you were asleep. What is it that you said? Whatever it was, you are experiencing a strange repose. You are asleep with your eyes wide open. You are standing, speaking, and moving, and yet you are fast asleep."

"Noble Sebastian, you are letting your fortune sleep — or, more accurately, you are letting it die. You are awake, but your eyes are closed."

Sebastian replied, "Antonio, you are snoring articulately — your snores have meaning."

"I am more serious than I customarily am," Antonio said. "You must be very serious, too, if you want to heed me. If you listen to me and do what I tell you to do, you will become much more powerful than you are now. You can jump over Alonso, Ferdinand, and Claribel to become the King of Naples."

"I am waiting for you to explain things more clearly," Sebastian said. "It is as if I am water that stands still. I am not inclined to move one way or another."

"I'll teach you how to flow," Antonio said.

"Do so," Sebastian said. "As a younger brother, I have been forced to be idle and so I know how to ebb. I decline, rather than increase. Younger brothers inherit little."

"Your words mock ambition, but I know that you are ambitious," Antonio said. "The more you mock ambition, the more you cherish it. Ebbing men, indeed, decline and stay at the bottom because of their fear or sloth. To change your fortune and cease to be a declining man, you must not be afraid or indolent."

"Please, say more," Sebastian said. "Your eyes and face tell me that you have something important to say, but they also tell me that it takes an effort to openly and clearly say it."

"Let me speak openly and clearly," Antonio replied.

He pointed to Gonzalo and said, "Although this Lord of weak memory, who shall be little remembered after he has been buried, has almost persuaded King Alonso that Ferdinand, his son, is still alive — Gonzalo is a spirit of persuasion because his job is to offer advice — it is as impossible for Ferdinand to still be alive as it is that Gonzalo here is awake and swimming."

"Ferdinand has definitely drowned," Sebastian said. "It is impossible for him to have safely reached this island. There is no hope that he safely reached land."

"Out of that 'no hope' comes great hope for you! No hope that Ferdinand is alive is so high a hope that you can become King of Naples that even the most ambitious man cannot hope for more without doubting that what it hopes for is unreal. Do you really believe — as do I — that Ferdinand has drowned?"

"He is dead and gone," Sebastian said.

"Then, tell me, who is the next heir of the King of Naples?"

"Claribel."

"Claribel is Queen of Tunis," Antonio said. "She dwells in a place that is 30 miles more than the journey of a lifetime. She can receive no news from Naples unless the Sun itself carries a letter to her — the Man in the Moon is too slow because the Moon takes a month rather than a day to complete its cycle. Any letter she receives will be written when a baby boy is born and delivered when the boy begins to shave his beard. Who will undertake to deliver that letter? Claribel is the woman from whom we were sailing when we were swallowed by the sea, though some of us were cast up on shore because we are destined to perform an act whose prologue is the recent past: the tempest and the shipwreck. The future is the part that you and I will play."

Antonio had exaggerated the distance between Tunis and Naples. In reality, 300 miles lay between the two cities, and merchant ships regularly engaged in trade between Italy and North Africa.

"What stuff and nonsense is this! What are you saying?" Sebastian said. "It is true that my brother's daughter is the Queen of Tunis; she is also the heir of the King of Naples. It is also true that between Tunis and Naples is a great space."

"It is a space whose every inch seems to cry out, 'How can Claribel travel back to Naples? Let her stay in Tunis, and let Sebastian wake himself up and enjoy his good fortune.' For a moment, imagine that these sleeping men had been seized by death — they would be no worser off than they are now. Other people can rule Naples as well as this King who sleeps. Other Lords can prate as amply and unnecessarily as this Gonzalo; I myself could make a jackdaw chatter as profoundly as Gonzalo. I wish that you thought the way that I do! The sleep of these men can lead to your advancement — you can become King of Naples! Do you understand me?"

"I think I do," Sebastian said.

"And what do you think about your opportunity? Are you willing to take action to make your fortune?"

"I remember that you supplanted your brother: Prospero. You drove him out of Milan and seized his title: Duke of Milan."

"True," Antonio said, "and look how well my garments sit upon me; they fit me much better than before. When my brother was Duke of Milan, his servants were my fellows; now they are my servants."

"What about your conscience?"

"What about it?" Antonio said. "If my conscience were a sore on my heel, it would make me wear soft slippers, but my conscience does not bother me. If twenty consciences lay between me and my becoming Duke of Milan, all twenty consciences would have to be coated with sugar and then softened by compassion before they would bother me. Here in front of you lies your brother; he is no better than the earth he lies upon. We can get rid of the people who stand in your way. I, using only three inches of the obedient steel of my sword, can put your brother at everlasting rest. You can do similarly to this ancient morsel, this Sir Prudence, this Gonzalo. As for the other Lords, they will do and say whatever we tell them to do and say as eagerly as a cat laps up milk. They will agree to anything we propose — they will say that the time is whatever we say it is."

Sebastian made up his mind to murder his brother.

He said to Antonio, "Your biography, my friend, shall be my precedent. The way that you became Duke of Milan is the way that I will become King of Naples. Draw your sword. With one stroke, you will kill my brother. Your reward will be that you and Milan will no longer have to pay tribute to the King of Naples and that I the new King will be your ally."

"Let us draw our swords together, and when I rear my hand and sword, you do the same thing. I will kill your brother the King, and you will kill Gonzalo."

They drew their swords, but Sebastian said, "Just a moment. I have something to say."

As Sebastian and Antonio talked quietly, Ariel flew to the group of men. He said over the sleeping Gonzalo, "Prospero, my master, has used magic to foresee the danger that you, his friend, are in. He has sent me forth — because otherwise his plan will fail — to keep you and the King of Naples alive."

Ariel sang this song in Gonzalo's ear:

"*While you here do snoring lie,*

"*Open-eyed conspiracy*

"*His opportunity does take.*

"*If for your life you have a care,*

"*Shake off slumber, and beware:*

"*Awake, awake!*"

Antonio said, "Let us both act quickly."

Gonzalo — the only one who could hear Ariel, and even he could not hear Ariel distinctly — woke up, saw Sebastian and Antonio with their drawn swords, shook the King to wake him, and shouted, "Now, good angels preserve the King!"

King Alonso woke up and asked Sebastian and Antonio, "What is going on? Why have you drawn your swords? Why do you look so frightened?"

Gonzalo asked, "What's the matter?"

Sebastian thought quickly and then lied to his brother, the King, "While we stood here and guarded you as you slept, just now we heard a loud burst of bellowing like bulls, or rather lions. Didn't it wake you? The bellowing struck my ears most terribly."

"I heard nothing," King Alonso said.

Antonio said, "Oh, it was a din to frighten a monster's ears or to make the earth tremble like an earthquake! Surely, it was the roar of a whole herd of lions."

"Did you hear this roaring, Gonzalo?"

"Upon my honor, sir, I heard a humming, and that a strange humming, too, which woke me," Gonzalo said. "As my eyes opened and I saw their weapons drawn, I shook you, sir, and cried out. There was a noise — that is certain. It is best that we stay upon our guard, or that we leave this place. Let's draw our weapons."

King Alonso said, "Lead us away from this ground, and let's make a further search for my poor son, in case he is still alive."

"May Heaven protect him and keep him away from these beasts!" Gonzalo said. "I am sure that your son is on the island."

"Lead us away from here," King Alonso said again.

As they left, Ariel thought, *Prospero, who is my Lord, shall know what I have done. So, King Alonso, go safely on to seek your son.*

— 2.2 —

Caliban was carrying wood on another part of the island when he heard thunder.

"May all the infections that the Sun sucks up from bogs, waterlands, and swamps fall on Prospero and make him inch by inch a walking disease! I know his spirits hear me, and yet I must curse him. But his spirits will not torment me, frighten me with goblins that have assumed the form of hedgehogs, throw me in the mire, or lead me, like a torch, in the dark out of my way, unless Prospero orders them to. Still, for my every trifling offense Prospero sets them upon me. Sometime the spirits are like apes that make faces and chatter at me and then bite me. Sometimes the spirits are like porcupines that lie in my way as I walk barefooted. Sometimes the spirits are like snakes that wind themselves around me and hiss at me with their cloven tongues and drive me insane."

Caliban saw Trinculo, the jester of King Alonso, walking toward him.

Caliban said, "Look, now, look! Here comes one of Prospero's spirits to torment me because I am bringing in this wood so slowly. I will lie flat on the ground and cover myself with my cloak. Perhaps the spirit will not see and bother me."

Trinculo said, "Here I see neither bush nor shrub that will shelter me from bad weather, and I know that another storm is brewing. I hear the storm sing in the wind. That black cloud yonder — it's huge — looks like a foul bottle that would like to bombard me with its liquid or like a cannon that would like to bombard me with its hail of cannonballs. If this storm should thunder the way it did before, I don't know where to hide my head. That cloud cannot do otherwise but shed rain by pailfuls."

Trinculo looked down, saw Caliban, and said, "What have we here? Is it a man or a fish? Is it dead or alive? It is a fish. It smells like a fish; it has a very ancient and fish-like smell — a smell not of the freshest fish. It is a strange fish! Were I in England now, as once I was, and I had this fish painted on a sign and I exhibited this fish, every fool on holiday there would pay me a piece of silver to see this fish. In England, this monster would make a man monetarily wealthy. In fact, in England this fish might be mistaken for a man — any strange beast there makes a man. Although many Englishmen will not give a dime in charity to relieve a lame beggar, they will pay out ten times as much to see a dead Indian."

Trinculo looked closely at Caliban and said, "This fish has legs like a man, and this fish's fins are like arms!"

He touched Caliban and said, "He is warm! I think I was mistaken. This is no fish; instead, this is an islander who was recently hit by lightning."

Thunder sounded.

Trinculo said, "The storm has come again! My best course of action is to creep under this islander's cloak; no other shelter is available. Misery acquaints a man with strange bedfellows. I will here shroud myself with this cloak until the dregs of the storm have passed over me."

Stephano, the King of Naples' butler, walked toward Caliban and Trinculo. He had a bottle of wine in his hand, and he was drunk.

He sang this song:

"I shall go no more to sea, to sea,

"Here shall I die ashore —"

He stopped and then said, "This is a very scurvy tune to sing at a man's funeral. Well, this bottle is my comfort."

He lifted the bottle and drank from it, and then he continued to sing:

"The master, the swabber, the boatswain and I,

"The gunner and his mate

"Loved Mall, Meg, and Marian and Margery,

"But none of us cared for Kate;

"For she had a tongue with a tang,

"Would cry to a sailor, 'Go hang!'

"She loved not the smell of tar or of pitch,

He stopped singing and then said, "'A tailor might scratch her wherever she itched' — she did not like real men such as sailors but instead preferred effeminate men such as tailors. Well, as long as her sexual itch gets scratched, she's happy. This is a scurvy tune, too, but this bottle is my comfort."

He drank again.

Trinculo had heard Stephano's voice. He was afraid that it was the voice of a devil, and so he trembled. This frightened Caliban, who thought that a spirit was tormenting him and so moaned, "Do not torment me! Please!"

Hearing Caliban, Stephano looked down, saw the cloak (from which four legs were protruding), and said, "What's the matter? Have we devils here? Are you devils playing tricks on me by showing me savages and men of the West Indies? I have not escaped drowning to be afraid now of your four legs. An old expression states this: As good a man as ever went on four legs cannot make him retreat. It shall continue to be stated as long as Stephano breathes through his nostrils. I am afraid of no man, including no four-legged man."

Trinculo continued to tremble, and Caliban moaned, "The spirit torments me!"

Stephano saw the trembling and said, "This is some monster of the island with four legs, who is, I believe, shivering from a fever. He speaks English, but where the devil did he learn our language? I will give him some relief, if only because he speaks English. If I can cure him and tame him and get to Naples with him, I will give him as a present — provided I receive a royal reward — to any emperor who has ever trod on shoes made of leather."

Caliban said, "Do not torment me, please. I'll bring my wood home faster."

Stephano said, "He's having a fit now and does not talk like a wise man. He shall drink wine from my bottle. If he has never drunk wine before, it is likely to stop his fit. If I can cure him of his fever and keep him tame, I will not sell him cheaply — too much money will not be enough. Whoever wants to buy him shall pay for him — and pay well."

Caliban said, "So far you have hurt me only a little, but I know that you will hurt me more. I can tell by your trembling that Prospero is giving you orders to hurt me."

Stephano uncovered Caliban's head and said, "Come on and open your mouth. I have something that will give you language, cat. You know the old proverb: Ale will make a cat speak. Open your mouth and drink; this will shake your shaking from fever, I can promise you, and it will do that quickly and thoroughly."

Caliban drank, but never having tasted wine before, it tasted strange to him and he spit it out.

Stephano said, "You don't know who your friends are. Open your mouth again."

Trinculo said, "I should know that voice. I recognize it. It belongs to — but he drowned, and this is a devil who is speaking! Help me, God!"

"Four legs and two voices: a most cunningly made monster!" Stephano said. "The purpose of his forward voice is to speak well of his friend; the purpose of his backward voice is to utter foul and insulting speeches. He resembles the figure of

Fame. If all the wine in my bottle will cure him, I will cure his illness. Amen! I will pour some wine in your other mouth."

"Stephano!" Trinculo cried.

"Does your other mouth call me?" Stephano said. "Mercy, mercy! This is a devil, and no monster. I will leave him; I have no long spoon, and he who will eat with the devil must have a long spoon."

"Stephano!" Trinculo shouted. "If you are Stephano, touch me to show me that you are not a devil and then speak to me, for I am Trinculo — don't be afraid. I am your good friend Trinculo."

"If you are Trinculo, come forth," Stephano said. "I will pull this monster's lesser legs. If any of this monster's four legs are Trinculo's legs, these are they."

He pulled Trinculo out from underneath Caliban's cloak — and from between Caliban's legs — and said, "You really are Trinculo indeed! How did you come to be a turd of this Mooncalf? Can this Mooncalf shit Trinculos?"

Mooncalves are misshapen monstrosities. The Moon is sometimes thought to be not always a benign influence.

Trinculo replied, "I thought that he was an islander who was killed by a thunderbolt. But you are not drowned, Stephano? I hope that you are not drowned. And has the storm blown over us? I hid myself under the dead Mooncalf's cloak because I was afraid of the storm. But you are alive, Stephano. Two Neapolitans have escaped drowning!"

Trinculo danced around Stephano with happiness and jostled him.

"Please, do not bump into me," Stephano said. "My stomach is not settled."

"These are fine things, if they are not spirits. That is a splendid god and he carries celestial liquor," Caliban said to himself. "I will kneel to him."

Caliban's first taste of wine had not been Heavenly to him, but a few swallows had made him like wine.

Stephano asked Trinculo, "How did you escape? How did you come to be here? Swear by this bottle that you will truly tell me how you came to be here. I myself escaped upon a barrel of sack — Spanish Canary wine — that the sailors heaved overboard. I swear that by this bottle, which I made from the bark of a tree with my own hands after I was cast ashore."

"I'll swear upon that bottle to be your true subject," Caliban said. "The liquor in that bottle is not Earthly."

Stephano ignored Caliban and said to Trinculo, "Here. Take the bottle. Swear upon it to tell me truly how you escaped being drowned."

"I swam ashore, man, like a duck," Trinculo said. "I can swim like a duck — I will swear to that."

"Here, kiss the book," Stephano said.

People sometimes kiss the book — the Bible — to confirm an oath. Stephano had no Bible, but he did have a bottle of wine. By 'kiss the book,' he meant for Trinculo to confirm his oath by taking a drink of wine from the bottle.

Stephano added, "Though you can swim like a duck, you look like a goose."

Trinculo drank some wine, and then he asked, "Oh, Stephano, do you have any more of this?"

"I have a whole barrel of it," Stephano said. "My wine cellar is in a rocky cave by the seaside — that is where I hid my wine."

He then said to Caliban, "How are you, Mooncalf! Are you recovering from your illness?"

"Did you drop from the Heavens?" Caliban asked.

"I dropped from the Moon, I assure you," Stephano joked. "Once upon a time, I was the Man in the Moon."

Caliban replied, "I have seen you on the Moon, and I do adore you. My female teacher showed me you and your dog and your bush."

Miranda had taught Caliban the story about how the man became the Man in the Moon. He, accompanied by his dog, was gathering firewood — dry bushes — on Sunday. This was a sin, and as punishment for that sin, he, his dog, and the wood he had gathered were placed on the Moon.

"Come, swear to that," Stephano said, "Kiss the book. Don't worry. I will furnish it soon with new contents. Swear on the book."

Trinculo said, "In this good light provided by the Sun, I can see the monster clearly, and I can see that he is not a deep thinker — this is a simple-minded monster. I cannot believe that I was afraid of him! He is a very weak-in-mind monster! He believed that you are the Man in the Moon! He is a very poor and credulous monster!"

Caliban drank, and Trinculo said, "Well done! That was a mighty long drink, monster!"

Caliban said to Stephano, "I will show you every fertile inch of the island, and I will kiss your foot. Please, be my god."

"He is a very perfidious and drunken monster! When his god is asleep, he will steal his wine."

"I will kiss your foot," Caliban said to Stephano. "I will swear to be your subject."

"Come on then," Stephano said. "Get down on your knees, and swear."

Trinculo said, "I shall laugh myself to death at this puppy-headed monster. He is a most scurvy monster! I could find in my heart to beat him —"

Stephano gave Caliban the bottle and said to him, "Come, kiss the bottle."

"— except that the poor monster is drunk. He is an abominable monster!"

Books had already mastered Caliban: Prospero's books of magic. Now he was being mastered by another "book": Stephano's bottle of wine.

Caliban said to Stephano, "I will show you the best springs; I will pluck berries for you. I will fish for you and I will get firewood for you. A plague upon the tyrant whom I serve! I will carry no more sticks to him, but instead I will follow you, you wondrous man."

"He is a most ridiculous monster — he is calling a poor drunkard 'wondrous'!" Trinculo said.

"Please," Caliban said, "let me bring you where crabs shed their shells and grow new ones. I with my long nails will dig peanuts for you. I will show you a jay's nest and I will teach you how to snare the nimble marmoset monkey. I will lead you to clustering hazelnuts, and sometimes I will get for you young birds that nest in the rocks. Will you go with me?"

"Yes," Stephano said. "Lead the way without any more talking." He added, "Trinculo, since the King and all the people we traveled with have drowned, we will inherit this island."

Stephano said to Caliban, "Carry my bottle."

Caliban sang drunkenly, "*Farewell, master; farewell, farewell!*"

Trinculo said, "This is a howling monster; he is a drunken monster!"

Caliban sang, "*No more dams I'll make for catching fish,*
"*Nor fetch in firewood*
"*On request.*
"*Nor scrape wooden platters, nor wash dishes.*
"*'Ban, 'ban, Ca-Caliban*
"*Has a new master. My old master can get a new man.*
"*Freedom, hey-day! Hey-day, freedom!*
"*Freedom, hey-day, freedom!*"

Stephano said, "Oh, fine monster! Lead the way!"

Stephano and Trinculo followed Caliban.

CHAPTER 3

— 3.1 —

Ferdinand was busy doing the task that Prospero had given to him: moving pieces of logs, which would be used for firewood.

He put down the wood he was carrying and said to himself, "I am a nobleman, and noblemen are not supposed to do hard physical labor. Some jobs take effort, but the delight we get from them outweighs the effort. Some kinds of base jobs are nobly undertaken; even the poorest jobs can have rich ends. Although I am a nobleman, my job now is carrying wood. This mean task would be as wearisome to me as it is odious, except that the young woman whom I serve gives life to what is dead and turns my labors into pleasures. Oh, she is ten times gentler in temper than her father is sour in temper — and he is composed of harshness. My job is to move thousands of pieces of logs and pile them up — Prospero has harshly ordered me to do this job. The sweet young woman whom I just met but whom I love weeps when she sees me work, and she says that such a demeaning task was never performed by such a person as I am. But I had better get back to work and stop daydreaming."

He picked up the wood and said, "These sweet thoughts refresh me as I work. Still, although my thoughts are sweet while I work, they are even sweeter and come to me in greater number when I take a break from work."

Miranda now walked up to Ferdinand. Behind her was Prospero. He was invisible, and neither Miranda nor Ferdinand knew that he was present.

Miranda said to Ferdinand, "Please, do not work so hard. I wish that the lightning had burned up those pieces of logs that my father ordered you to pile up! Please, set the wood down and rest. When this wood burns, the resin that seeps out will be tears shed in repentance for having wearied you. My father is hard at study; please, rest for a while. He will be busy for the next three hours."

"Dear young woman," Ferdinand said, "the Sun will set before I shall finish the job that your father ordered me to do."

"If you'll sit down," Miranda said, "I'll carry your wood for you for a while. Please, give me that wood. I will carry it to the pile."

"No, precious lady," Ferdinand said. "I prefer to crack my sinews and break my back rather than allow you to undergo such dishonor while I lazily sit and watch you."

Miranda replied, "This work is as appropriate for me as it is for you, and I would do it with much more ease because I want to help you and you would prefer not to do demeaning work."

Prospero thought, *Poor lass, if love is a disease, you have been infected! This visit of yours to Ferdinand shows it.*

"You look tired," Miranda said to Ferdinand.

"No, noble lady. It is fresh morning with me when you are nearby at night. I do ask you — mainly so that I can mention you in my prayers — what is your name?"

"Miranda — oh, my father told me not to tell you my name!"

"Admired Miranda! 'Miranda' means 'to be admired.' Indeed, you are the top of admiration! You are worth what is most valuable to the world! Very many ladies I have eyed with highest approval, and many a time the harmony of their tongues has brought into bondage my too attentive ear. I have liked several women for their various virtues, but never has any of these women had a perfect soul. Always some defect in her quarreled with the noblest virtue she had and defeated it. But you, Miranda, you are so perfect and so peerless — you are created out of the best qualities of every created being!"

"I have never known a woman, and I can remember no woman's face except for my own, which I see in the mirror. Nor have I seen any men except for you, good friend, and my dear father. What people elsewhere look like I do not know, but I swear by my modesty and my chastity, which are the best jewels in my dowry, that I do not wish any companion in the world but you, and I cannot even imagine a man, besides yourself, whom I would like. But I prattle too wildly and I forget what my father has ordered me not to say and do."

"I am a Prince, Miranda," Ferdinand said. "I think, in fact, that I am now a King although I would prefer my father to still be alive and still be King! Except that I am forced by your father's magic to endure this slavery of carrying wood, I would tolerate it no more than I would tolerate a fly's laying its eggs in my mouth the way a flesh-fly lays its eggs on rotten meat. Hear me speak from my soul: The very instant that I saw you, my heart flew to serve you and be your slave. For your sake, I endure patiently this work of carrying wood."

"Do you love me?" Miranda asked.

"May Heaven and Earth listen to what I say and give me good fortune if I speak truly! If I lie, then invert whatever good should come to me and make it evil! I love, prize, and honor you more than everything else in this world."

Miranda cried and said, "I am a fool to weep because of what makes me happy."

Prospero said to himself, "This is a beautiful encounter of two exceptional loves. May the Heavens rain grace on the love that is developing between them!"

"Why are you crying?" Ferdinand asked.

Miranda replied, "I am crying because I am not worthy to give you what I want to give you, and because I am unworthy to take what I am dying to have. But I am speaking in riddles: All the more it seeks to hide itself, the bigger bulk it shows."

Prospero thought, *My daughter's words have sexual meanings. She has grown up. All the more a penis seeks to hide itself in a vagina, the bigger bulk it shows.*

Miranda continued, "Go away, bashful cunning! Let plain and holy innocence give me words and allow me to speak openly! I am your wife, if you will marry me; if you will not marry me, I will die your maiden. You may keep me from being your wife, but I will be your servant, whether or not you want me to be."

In this society, a "servant" can be a person who loves someone.

"You may command me, lady, and I kneel humbly before you."

"You will be my husband, then?" Miranda asked.

"Yes, and with a heart as eager as a slave is to be free. Take my hand."

They held hands.

"My heart is also as eager to marry you," Miranda said.

In this society, people became engaged by holding hands and agreeing to marry each other.

She then said, "And now farewell until half an hour from now."

"A thousand thousand farewells!" Ferdinand said.

Ferdinand and Miranda left in different directions.

Prospero said to himself, "I cannot be as glad of this as they are — they were taken by surprise at their falling in love, but I was expecting it. Still, nothing can give me greater pleasure than this. I will go to my magic books, for before suppertime I must perform many things related to this."

— 3.2 —

On another part of the island, Caliban, Stephano, and Trinculo were still talking and drinking.

"Don't criticize me," Stephano said to Trinculo, who had wanted him to moderate his drinking. "When the barrel of wine is empty, we will drink water, but not a drop before. Therefore, bear up, stand firm, and lift the bottle, and then board 'em and attack — drink! Servant-monster, drink to me."

"Servant-monster!" Trinculo said. "He is the folly of this island! Only five people are on this island; we are three of them. If the other two have drunken brains like ours, this island is in a terrible state and its inhabitants are in a tottering state."

"Drink, servant-monster, when I tell you to," Stephano said. "Your eyes are almost drunkenly set in your head."

"Where else should his eyes be set?" Trinculo said. "He would be a splendid monster, indeed, if they were set in his tail."

"My man-monster has drowned his tongue with wine," Stephano said, "As for me, the sea cannot drown me. I swam, before I could reach the shore, thirty-five leagues — around 100 miles — by fits and starts."

Trinculo thought, *That may be a slight exaggeration.*

Stephano said to Caliban, "By Heaven, you will be my military lieutenant, monster, or my standard-bearer."

Trinculo said, "You better make him your lieutenant. Because of the wine he has drunk, he is not capable of standing."

Trinculo was punning. An erection is one kind of standing, and as all know, alcohol increases desire but takes away performance.

He added, "But if you enlist him as your lieutenant, he will list to one side like a damaged ship."

Stephano said, "We will not run away from the enemy, Monsieur Monster."

"Nor go — walk — either," Trinculo said, "but you'll lie like dogs and yet say nothing."

"Mooncalf, speak once in your life," Stephano said, "if you are a good Mooncalf."

"How are you, sir?" Caliban said. "Let me lick your shoe. I will not serve Trinculo; he's not valiant."

"You lie, most ignorant monster," Trinculo said. "I am drunk enough to shove a constable. Why, you debauched fish, has ever a man been a coward who has drunk as much wine as I have drunk today? Why are you telling a monstrous lie, you who are only half a monster? Which of us is valiant? I drink like an entire fish, but you are only half a fish."

"Listen at how he mocks me!" Caliban said to Stephano. "Will you let him mock me, my Lord?"

"He called Stephano 'Lord'!" Trinculo said. "I am amazed that a monster should be such a natural fool! Monsters are unnatural!"

"Listen! He mocked me again!" Caliban complained. "Please bite him to death."

"Trinculo, keep a civil tongue in your head," Stephano said. "If you mutiny against me, I will hang you from the nearest tree! The poor monster is my subject, and he shall not suffer indignity."

"I thank my noble Lord," Caliban said. "Will you be pleased to listen once again to the petition I made to you?"

Petitions are made to Princes; petitions often ask for redress of wrongs. Stephano and Caliban now began to act as if they were in a royal court and Stephano was a Prince.

Stephano said, "Yes, I will. Kneel before me, and repeat your petition. I will stand up, and so will Trinculo."

Ariel, invisible, now came near the three drunks. He stood behind Trinculo, who was a short distance from Caliban and Stephano.

Caliban said to Stephano, "As I told you before, I am subject to a tyrant, a sorcerer, who by his cunning has cheated me out of this island."

"You lie!" Ariel said.

Because Ariel was standing behind Trinculo — who could not hear Ariel, who had the power of making sounds, including music, audible only to the people he chose to hear them — and because Ariel was invisible, Caliban and Stephano assumed that Trinculo had said, "You lie!"

Caliban angrily said to Trinculo, "*You* lie, you jesting monkey! I wish my valiant master would destroy you! *I* do not lie."

Stephano said, "Trinculo, if you trouble him any more as he tells his tale, I swear that I will uproot some of your teeth."

"Why, I said nothing," Trinculo protested.

"Be quiet, then, and say no more," Stephano said.

To Caliban, he added, "Proceed."

"I say, by sorcery he got this island. From me he got it. If your greatness will get revenge on him for what he did to me — I know that you are valiant enough to do that, but I am not —"

"That's quite certain," Stephano said.

Caliban finished, "— you shall be Lord of this island and I will serve you."

"How can we accomplish that?" Stephano said. "Can you take me to this magician?"

"Yes, my Lord," Caliban said. "I will take you to him while he is asleep. Then you can hammer a nail into his head."

Ariel said, "You lie! You cannot do that!"

Again, Caliban and Stephano assumed that Trinculo the jester had spoken.

"What a pied ninny is this!" Caliban said, referring to the jester's clothing made of patches of different colors — a style called pied or motley. You scurvy patch!"

Caliban was capable — occasionally — of wit. The word "patch" referred to the jester's clothing made of patches — "patch" also meant "fool, clown, simpleton," words that described Trinculo well. In fact, events would show that Caliban was more intelligent than either Trinculo or Stephano.

Caliban said to Stephano, "I do beg your greatness, give this fool blows and take his bottle from him. When his bottle is gone, he shall drink nothing but brine water because I will not show him where the springs of fresh water are."

"Trinculo, run into no further danger," Stephano, who was a bit of a bully, said. "Interrupt the monster one word further, and, by this hand, I will fire my mercy the way we fire a servant and turn it out of doors, and I will treat you like a salted fish — I will beat you in order to tenderize you."

"Why, what did I do?" Trinculo complained. "I did nothing. I'll go farther away from you."

Stephano asked him, "Didn't you say that the monster lied?"

Ariel said, "You lie!"

"I lie?" Stephano said. "Do I now? Take that."

He hit Trinculo and said, "If you like this, then tell me once more that I lied."

"I did not call you a liar," Trinculo protested. "Are you out of your mind? Are you deaf? A pox on your bottle! Wine and drinking can make people act like you! May your monster catch the plague, and may the devil take your fingers!"

Caliban laughed at Trinculo's discomfort.

"Now, monster, go forward with your tale," Stephano said.

He said to Trinculo, "Please, stand farther away."

"Beat him up," Caliban said. "After a little while, I'll beat him, too."

"Stand farther away," Stephano said to Trinculo. To Caliban, he said, "Come on, proceed. Tell me what you have to tell me."

"Why, as I told you," Caliban said, "it is a custom with him to sleep in the afternoon. At that time, you can brain him, after you have seized his magic books, or you can use a piece of wood to batter his skull in, or you can stab him with a stake. Or you can cut his throat with your knife. Remember first to take his magic books because without them he is only a fool, as I am, and he will not be able to command any spirits

— they hate him as deeply as I do. Burn only his books. He has fine furnishings — so he calls them — with which he intends to adorn his house, when he has a proper one. Those fine furnishings will be yours. But even more important is that you can win his daughter, who is beautiful. The magician himself calls her a nonpareil — her beauty is supposed to be without equal. I never have seen a woman except for two: Sycorax, who was my dam, and the magician's daughter, who as far surpasses Sycorax in beauty as the greatest surpasses the least."

"Is she so splendid a lass?" Stephano asked.

"Yes, Lord," Caliban replied. "She will look good in your bed — I guarantee it — and she will give birth to splendid children for you."

Caliban had cleverly pointed out the benefits Stephano would receive if he killed Prospero.

"Monster, I will kill this man," Stephano said. "His daughter and I will be King and Queen — God save our graces! — and Trinculo and you shall be viceroys."

He added, "Do you like the plot, Trinculo?"

"Excellently."

"Let's shake hands," Stephano said to Trinculo. "I am sorry I hit you, but as long as you are alive, keep a good tongue in your head. Don't insult the monster or me."

"Within this half hour, the magician will be asleep," Caliban said. "Will you destroy him then?"

"Yes, on my honor," Stephano replied.

Ariel thought, *I will tell my master about this plot.*

Caliban said, "You make me happy. I am full of pleasure. Let us be jocund. Will you sing the song that you taught me recently?"

"At your request, monster," Stephano said, "I will do anything within reason. Come on, Trinculo, let us sing."

Stephano and Trinculo sang this song:

"*Flout 'em and jeer at 'em*

"*And jeer at 'em and flout 'em*

"*Thought is free.*"

They were drunk and sang poorly, and Caliban complained, "That's not the tune."

Ariel began to play the tune with his small drum and wind instrument.

"What is this sound?" Stephano asked.

"This is the tune of our song, played by the picture of Nobody," Trinculo said.

Ariel was invisible, and so he was Nobody because he had no body.

"If you are a man, show yourself in your true shape," Stephano said. "If you are a devil, then I challenge you to a duel."

Afraid that the devil was willing to accept the invitation to fight a duel, Trinculo said, "Oh, God, forgive me my sins!"

Stephano said, "He who dies pays all debts. I defy you, devil."

Drunk Stephano then realized that he had mixed his words up. He should have challenged the man to a duel and asked the devil to appear in his true shape. Challenging a devil to a duel is not a good idea.

Stephano cried, "God, have mercy upon us!"

"Are you afraid?" Caliban asked him, thinking that he was afraid of the music.

Not wanting to appear to be a coward in front of Caliban, Stephano replied, "No, monster, not I."

Not convinced, Caliban replied, "Be not afraid. This island is full of noises, sounds, and sweet airs that give delight and do not hurt. Sometimes a thousand twangling instruments will hum about my ears, and sometimes I hear voices that, if I then had waked after a long sleep, will make me sleep again, and then, as I dreamed, I thought that the clouds would open up and show me riches that were about to drop upon me — when I woke up, I cried because I wanted to dream again."

"This will prove a splendid kingdom to me, where I shall have my music for free," Stephano said.

"After Prospero the magician is destroyed," Caliban said.

"That shall be soon," Stephano said. "I have not forgotten."

"The music is going away," Trinculo said. "Let's follow it, and afterward kill the magician."

"Lead, monster; we'll follow," Stephano said. "I wish that I could see this musician; he plays well."

Caliban hung back. He wanted to kill the magician first.

"Are you coming?" Trinculo asked Caliban. He said to Stephano, "I will follow you, Stephano."

Stephano and Trinculo left. Caliban followed them.

— 3.3 —

King Alonso, Sebastian, Antonio, Gonzalo, Adrian, Francisco, and others had been walking, searching for King Alonso's son, Ferdinand. Sebastian and Antonio stood at a distance from the other men.

"I can go no further, sir," Gonzalo said. "My old bones ache. Here is a maze trod indeed through straight paths and winding ways. Please, sir, I must rest."

"Old Lord, I cannot blame you for wanting to rest," King Alonso said. "I also am worn with weariness, and my spirits have dulled. Sit down, and rest. Now I will stop hoping that my son is alive; I will no longer try to comfort myself with the thought that he may have survived. No, he did not survive. My son, whom we are searching for, has drowned. The sea mocks our useless search for him on land. Well, I will accept that he is dead."

Antonio whispered to Sebastian, "I am very glad that King Alonso has lost hope that his son is alive. He is depressed and discouraged. Do not, although we failed once to assassinate the King and Gonzalo, give up our plan that you agreed to."

Sebastian whispered back to Antonio, "We will seize by the throat the next opportunity we have to do what we planned."

Antonio whispered back, "Let it be tonight; now they are weary with walking, and they will not, and they cannot, use such vigilance as they do when they are fresh and rested."

Sebastian whispered, "Yes, tonight. We are agreed."

Solemn and strange music began to play, and Prospero, who was invisible, stood on a height, and watched the group of men as strange spirits brought a table and put on it a banquet as they danced as if to welcome King Alonso and the other men. The spirits gestured to the men to eat the banquet, and then the spirits left although the music continued to play.

"What harmony is this?" King Alonso asked. "My good friends, listen!"

"This is marvelous sweet music!" Gonzalo said.

"May the Heavens give us kind keepers!" King Alonso said. "What were these beings?"

"We have seen a living puppet show," Sebastian said sarcastically. "Now I will believe that unicorns exist, and I will believe that in Arabia on one tree, the phoenix' throne, one phoenix is right now reigning there. Only one phoenix exists at a time, and every 500 years it bursts into flame and then is resurrected as a young bird."

"I will believe in both of those mythological beings," Antonio said sarcastically, "and if anything else wants to be believed in, then let it come to me, and I will swear that it exists. I believe that travelers never lie, although fools at home condemn them."

Without sarcasm, Gonzalo said, "If I would report in Naples what I just saw with my own eyes, would the people there believe me? If I would say, I saw such islanders — certainly, this island has inhabitants — who, though they are of monstrous shape, yet you shall find that their manners are better and more charitable than the manners of many — make that most — of our human species."

Prospero thought, *Honest and old Lord, you have spoken truly because some of you humans present here and now are worse than devils.*

"I cannot stop marveling that such shapes, using gestures and sounds, are able to express, although they lack the use of speech, a kind of excellent silent communication," King Alonso said.

Prospero thought, *Keep your praise until the end. You may find that you have not received the welcome that you think you have.*

Francisco said, "They vanished strangely."

"That does not matter," Sebastian said, "since they have left their banquet behind. We have good appetites."

He asked King Alonso, his brother, "Will it please you to eat the banquet that is here?"

Afraid of the strange shapes that had brought the food, King Alonso said, "I will not eat that food."

Gonzalo advised him, "Truly, sir, you need not fear. When we were boys, who would believe that there were mountain-dwellers dew-lapped like bulls, whose throats had hanging from them wallets of flesh that are also known as goiters? Or who would believe that there existed men whose heads were in their breasts? But now that we are grown up, we find that one in five travelers brings us reports of having seen such people."

"I will eat some of this food," King Alonso decided, "even though it may be my last meal. That does not matter since I believe that the best part of my life is over now that my son has died. Brother, and my Lord the Duke of Milan, take the risk and eat, also."

Thunder sounded and lightning flashed. Ariel, who had changed his shape to that of a Harpy, a bird with the face of a woman, entered with two other spirits in the shape of Harpies. Harpies had befouled the food that Aeneas, the survivor of Troy who carried out his fate of going to Italy and becoming an important ancestor of the Romans, and his men had prepared on the Island of the Harpies during their wanderings around the Mediterranean. Ariel clapped his wings, and the food disappeared.

Still in the form of a Harpy, Ariel said to King Alonso, Sebastian, and Antonio, "You are three men of sin, whom Destiny, which has power over this lower world and what is in it, has caused the never-surfeited sea to belch you upon this island where men do not live because you do not deserve to live among men. I have made you insane, and men sometimes hang or drown themselves with their insane courage."

King Alonso, Sebastian, and Antonio — the only men who could hear Ariel — drew their swords.

Ariel continued, "You fools! I and my fellows are ministers of Fate. The elements, of which your swords are created, may as well try to wound the loud winds, or with mocked-at stabs kill the waters that close together again as soon they are parted. They are as likely to do that as to harm one filament of one of my feathers. My fellow ministers of Fate are likewise invulnerable. Even if you could hurt us, your swords are now too heavy for your strength and you can no longer lift them."

The three men dropped their now-too-heavy swords to the ground.

Ariel continued, "But remember — this is what I must tell you — that you three men deposed Prospero and cast him from Milan, throwing him and his innocent child, exposed to the elements, upon the sea, which has avenged your evil deed. Because of your foul deed, the higher powers, which delayed your punishment but did not forget it, have incensed the seas and shores and all the creatures against you. King Alonso, you have been bereft of your son. The higher powers have ordered me to inflict on you a lingering, gradual, and slow destruction that will be worse than any quick death can be. Slow destruction will follow you every step of your way.

The only way to escape the wraths of the higher powers, which otherwise will fall upon your heads, is for the three of you to repent your sins and to lead a life innocent of sin."

Amid thunder, Ariel and the two other spirits vanished.

Soft music played, and other spirits danced as they made mocking grimaces and gestures at the three sinners, and then the spirits carried out the table on which the food had been placed.

"You have splendidly acted the role of the Harpy, Ariel," Prospero said. "Your acting had grace, even as you spirited away the food. You left out nothing of what I commanded you to say in your speech, and the spirits — all of whom are lesser than you — who worked with you performed their roles excellently with great attention to detail. My high magic works, and these my enemies are all confused and distracted. They now are in my power, and in these fits I leave them, while I visit young Ferdinand, whom they think has drowned, and Miranda, whom both he and I love."

Prospero departed.

Gonzalo, who had not heard Ariel's speech, said to King Alonso, "In the name of something holy, sir, why do you stand here and seem utterly amazed?"

"Oh, it is monstrous, monstrous," King Alonso said. "I thought that the billows spoke and told me the name of Prospero; the winds did sing the name of Prospero to me, and the thunder, that deep and dreadful organ-pipe, pronounced the name of Prospero. In a bass voice, the winds and the waves have sung out the name of the man I wronged. Because of my sin, my son is bedded in the ooze at the bottom of the ocean. I will seek him deeper than ever any plummet has sounded and with him I will lie there in the muddy ooze."

King Alonso walked away.

Sebastian said, "If I can fight one fiend at a time, I will fight their legions one after another."

Antonio said to Sebastian, "I'll be your second in each fight."

Sebastian and Antonio walked after King Alonso.

Gonzalo said to the other Lords, "All three of them are desperate. Their great guilt for what they did to Prospero, like poison that is designed to work a great time after it is taken, now begins to bite them. I do beg those of you who have suppler joints, follow them swiftly and keep them from doing what their frenzy may provoke them to do."

Adrian said, "We will go. Follow after us."

Gonzalo and the other Lords followed King Alonso, Sebastian, and Antonio.

CHAPTER 4

— 4.1 —

Prospero was talking to Ferdinand and Miranda outside his dwelling.

He said to Ferdinand, "If I have too severely treated you, the compensation you will receive makes amends because I have given you here a third of my own life: the person for whom I live. Once again I give her to you. All the vexations I have put you through were only my trials of your love — you have wonderfully passed the tests. Here, before Heaven, I certify this my rich gift. Oh, Ferdinand, do not smile at me when I boast about her and show her off because you shall find that she will outstrip all praise and make it limp behind her."

"I do believe everything you say," Ferdinand said, "and I would believe it even if an oracle were to contradict it."

"Then take my daughter as my gift and as your own acquisition that you have deserved to win, but if you take her virginity before the sanctimonious ceremony of marriage has with full and holy rite been ministered, then Heaven will allow no sweet sprinklings of grace to fall to bless this marriage. Instead, barren hate, sour-eyed disdain, and discord shall bestrew your marriage bed. It will not be covered with flowers but with weeds so loathsome that you both shall hate it. Therefore, take heed. If you two behave properly, the torches of Hyman, god of marriage, that we light on your wedding day will burn clearly and with a good light — a good omen. But if you two do not behave properly, the torches of Hyman, god of marriage, that we light on your wedding day will create lots of smoke — a bad omen."

Ferdinand replied, "As I hope for quiet days, fine children, and long life, with such love as Miranda and I have between us now, I will not allow the murkiest den, the most opportune place, the strongest temptation to make me take your daughter's virginity before we are married. All of us have a good nature and a selfish nature. I will not allow the selfish part of my nature to take away the anticipation of that day's celebration of our marriage when I shall think either that Phoebus' steeds that draw the Sun-chariot have collapsed through overwork and so the daytime will never end or that Night is kept chained below the Earth's surface and so our wedding night will never arrive."

"Well spoken," Prospero said. "Sit and talk with her; she is your own."

Prospero then called Ariel to appear before him: "Ariel! My industrious servant, Ariel!"

Ariel appeared and said, "What does my powerful master want? Here I am."

"You and the lesser spirits performed your last task — the tantalizing banquet — well, and I must use you in such another trick. Go bring the other spirits, over whom I give you power, here. Tell them to be quick because I must show the eyes of this young couple an example of my magical art. I have promised to do so, and they expect it."

"Immediately?" Ariel asked.

"Yes, in the time it takes to wink."

Mischievously, Ariel said, "Before you can say 'come' and 'go,' and breathe twice and cry 'so, so,' each one, tripping on his toe, will be here in his place, showing off and making a funny face."

Ariel paused, then added, "Do you love me, master? No?"

"I love you dearly, my delicate Ariel," Prospero said, and then he added, "Do not approach until you hear me call."

"I understand," Ariel replied and then flew away.

Prospero said to Ferdinand, who was hugging Miranda, "Make sure that you are true to the words you said to me just now. Do not engage in heavy petting. Do not allow your passion to run free. The strongest oaths are straw when the fire in the blood is aroused. Indulge yourself less, or else say goodbye to your vow!"

"I promise you, sir, that the white, cold snow of Miranda's chastity cools the heat of my heart," Ferdinand replied. "I have taken your words to heart and will not take your daughter's virginity until she and I are married."

"That is good," Prospero said.

He then said, "Now come, my Ariel! Bring too many spirits with you — that is better than not bringing enough spirits. Appear promptly!"

He said to Ferdinand, "No talking — that will break the spell! Be all eyes and no tongue! Be silent."

Soft music played, and a spirit appeared who played the role of Iris, goddess of the rainbow and messenger of the gods and especially messenger of Juno, Queen of the gods.

Iris said, "Ceres, goddess of fertility and agriculture, you most bounteous lady, I have a message for you. Juno, the Queen of the gods, commands you to leave your rich fields of wheat, rye, barley, tares for fodder, oats, and peas; your grassy mountains, where live nibbling sheep, and flat meadows thatched with winter fodder to feed the sheep; your streams with shaped and reinforced banks, which wet and rainy April at your request adorns with flowers, to make cold virginal nymphs chaste crowns; and your thickets of broom bushes, whose shadow the rejected bachelor loves, having lost his girl; your pruned vineyard; and your seashore, sterile and rocky hard, where you yourself do take the air. Juno, whose watery arch — the rainbow — and messenger I am, with her sovereign grace commands you to leave these, and here on this plot of grass, in this very place, to come and play. Juno's peacocks fly and quickly pull her chariot here. Approach, rich Ceres, so you can entertain Juno."

Juno's chariot appeared in the sky.

Ceres arrived, stood by Iris, and said, "Hail, many-colored messenger, who never disobeys Juno, the wife of Jupiter, King of the gods. Iris, you with your saffron wings sprinkle honey-drops and refreshing showers upon my flowers, and with each end of your blue bow you crown my bushy acres and my bare plains, rich scarf to my proud earth. Why has your Queen summoned me here to this short-grassed green land?"

"She wants you to celebrate a contract of true love and freely bestow a gift on the blessed lovers."

"Tell me if you know, Heavenly rainbow, whether Venus or Cupid, her son, do now attend the Queen? Venus and Cupid plotted to help dusky Dis, god of the underworld, to kidnap and marry Persephone, my daughter, and so I shun their company."

"Don't be afraid," Iris replied. "You will not see them. I met Venus as her chariot cut the clouds as she flew towards Paphos. Her son was with her in her chariot drawn by doves. They had thought to put some wanton charm upon this man and maiden, Ferdinand and Miranda, who have vowed that they will not sleep together until Hymen's torch has been lit and they have been married. But Venus and Cupid plotted in vain. Mars' lustful mistress, Venus, has returned again; her spiteful son has broken his arrows. He swears that he will shoot no more arrows but will instead play with sparrows and simply be a boy."

Juno's chariot descended, and she walked over to Iris and Ceres.

Ceres said, "The highest Queen of state, great Juno, is coming. I know her by her gait."

Juno said to Ceres, "How is my bounteous sister? Go with me to bless these two, Ferdinand and Miranda, so that they may be prosperous and have fine children."

The two goddesses — played by spirits — began to sing to Ferdinand and Miranda.

Juno sang, "*Honor, riches, marriage-blessing,*

"*Long continuance of marriage, with children and love increasing,*

"*Hourly joys be always upon you!*

"*Juno sings her blessings upon you.*"

Ceres sang, "*Earth's increase, abundance plenty,*

"*Barns and granaries never empty,*

"*Vines and clustering bunches growing,*

"*Plants with goodly burden bowing.*

"*Always you shall have food and wines.*

"*Spring come to you at the farthest*

"*At the very end of harvest —*

"*Never a winter in your lives!*

"Scarcity and want shall shun you.

"Ceres' blessing thus is on you."

Ferdinand whispered, "This is a very majestic vision, and harmoniously charming."

He asked Prospero, "Am I right in thinking that these are spirits?"

"Yes," Prospero said. "They are spirits, whom by my art I have called from their homes to enact this masque."

Ferdinand said, "Let me live here forever. So rare and wonderful and wonder-working and wise a father-in-law makes this place Paradise."

Juno and Ceres whispered, and then they sent Iris on an errand.

Prospero said, "Now, silence! Juno and Ceres whispered seriously. Something more is coming. Hush, and be quiet, or else our spell is marred."

Iris said, "You nymphs, called Naiads, of the winding, wandering brooks, with your crowns woven of water lilies, have ever-harmless and -innocent looks. Leave your small-waved water channels and on this green land answer your summons. Juno commands you to come, chaste nymphs, and help to celebrate a contract of true love; do not be too late."

Some spirits in the form of water-nymphs entered.

Iris continued, "You sunburnt sicklemen, made weary by August labors, come here from the furrows and be merry. Make holiday. Put on your rye-straw hats and perform a country dance with these pure and innocent nymphs."

Some spirits dressed like reapers entered and danced gracefully with the nymphs, but Prospero suddenly remembered something.

He thought, *I forgot about that foul conspiracy of the beast Caliban and his confederates against my life. The time they appointed to carry out my murder has almost come.*

He broke the spell by speaking to the spirits: "Well done! Leave now! No more!"

The spirits reluctantly departed.

Ferdinand said to Miranda, "This is strange. Your father is strongly upset about something."

"Never until this day," Miranda replied, "have I seen him so overcome by anger."

Prospero, noticing Ferdinand looking at him, said, "You do look, my son, distressed and dismayed. Be cheerful, sir. Our revels now are ended. Our actors, as I told you before, were all spirits and have melted into air, into thin air.

"Like the baseless fabric of this vision, the cloud-capped towers, the gorgeous palaces, the solemn temples, the great globe itself, and all who live on the Earth, shall dissolve and, like this insubstantial pageant that has faded, leave not a wisp of ourselves behind. We are made of such stuff as dreams are made of, and our little life is ended with a sleep.

"Sir, I am vexed. Bear with my weakness. My brain is troubled. Be not disturbed by my infirmity. Please retire inside my dwelling and rest there. I will walk for a while to quiet my agitated mind."

"We wish you peace," both Ferdinand and Miranda said.

Prospero called Ariel: *Come with a thought. I thank you, Ariel, for this masque. Come.*

Ariel arrived.

"I know your thoughts," Ariel said. "What is your pleasure?"

"Spirit, we must prepare to meet Caliban."

"True, my commander," Ariel said. "When I played the role of Ceres, I thought to have reminded you of Caliban's plot, but I was afraid that I would anger you."

"Tell me again. Where did you leave these varlets?"

"As I told you, sir," Ariel said, "they were red hot with drinking. They were so full of valor that they smote the air because it was blowing in their faces and they beat the ground because it kissed their feet, and yet they always moved toward their project. Then I beat my drum, at the sound of which, like unbroken colts, they pricked up their ears, raised their eyelids, and lifted up their noses as if they smelled music. I charmed their ears so that like calves they followed my lowing music through thorny briers, sharp furzes, pricking gorse, and thorns, which entered their frail shins. Finally I left them up to their necks in the scum-covered pool in back of your dwelling. The water stinks more than their feet."

"This was well done, my flying bird," Prospero said. "Stay invisible for now. Go to my dwelling and find rich clothing and bring it here. I will use it as bait to catch these thieves."

"I go, I go," Ariel said as he flew away.

Prospero said to himself, "Caliban is a devil, a born devil, on whose nature nurture can never stick and on whom my pains to educate him, all of which were humanely undertaken, were all lost, quite lost. As his body grows uglier with age, so his mind grows uglier day by day. I will plague them all so much that they will roar with pain."

Ariel returned, carrying a load of rich clothing.

Prospero said, "Hang the clothing on the branches of this lime tree."

As they waited, Prospero and Ariel were invisible to others. Soon Caliban, Stephano, and Trinculo, all wet and stinking, arrived.

Caliban said, "Please, walk quietly, so that even a blind mole — that has excellent hearing — will not hear a foot fall. We are now near the magician's dwelling."

Stephano said, "Monster, your fairy, whom you say is a harmless fairy, has done little better than treat us as knaves. That spirit has played a dirty trick on us."

Trinculo complained, "Monster, I do stink like horse piss, because of which my nose is greatly offended."

"My nose is also offended," Stephano said. "Do you hear me, monster? If I should take a dislike to you, look out —"

"You would be a ruined monster," Trinculo said.

"My good Lord," Caliban said to Stephano, "give me your favor still. Be patient, for the prize I will bring you to will make you forget this mishap. Therefore, speak softly. All is still as hushed as midnight."

"Yes, but we lost our bottle in the pool —" Trinculo complained.

"There is not only disgrace and dishonor in that, monster, but an infinite loss," Stephano said.

"Losing the bottle of wine hurts me more than this wetting, but yet this is your 'harmless fairy,' monster," Trinculo complained.

"I will find my bottle and carry it away even if I have to be in the water over my ears," Stephano said.

"Please, my King, be quiet," Caliban said to Stephano. "Look, this is the mouth of the cave in which the magician dwells. Make no noise, and enter. Do that good evil — a murder — that may make this island forever your own, and make me, your Caliban, forever your foot-licker.”

“Give me your hand,” Stephano said. “I do begin to have bloody thoughts.”

Trinculo saw the rich clothing that was hung on the lime tree and sang this song:

“*King Stephen was and is a worthy peer.*
“*His breeches cost him but a crown;*
“*He held them sixpence all too dear.*
“*With that he called that tailor a lout.*”

Then he added, “Oh, King Stephano! Oh, peer! Oh, worthy Stephano! Look what a wardrobe is here for you!”

Caliban said, “Let the clothing alone, you fool; it is only trash.”

Trinculo replied, “Monster, we know what belongs in a secondhand clothing shop, and it is not this kind of clothing!”

Trinculo put on a cloak and said, “Oh, King Stephano!”

Stephano said, “Take off that cloak, Trinculo; by this hand, I swear that I will have that cloak.”

Fearing Stephano’s hand, Trinculo took off the cloak and handed it to Stephano, saying, “Your grace shall have it.”

Keeping his eyes on the prize, Caliban said, “May dropsy drown this fool named Trinculo! What do you mean to dote thus on such unnecessary baggage? Let it alone and do the murder first. If the magician awakes, from toe to crown he’ll mark our skins with torments and turn us into strange stuff.”

“Shut up, monster,” Stephano said. “Tree, or should I say clothesline, isn’t this my jacket?”

He removed the jacket from the tree and said, “Now is the jacket under the line. Now, jacket, you are likely to lose your fur lining through use and prove to be a bald jacket just like sailors traditionally have all their hair cut off when they for the first time cross the line that is the equator."

"That's the way to do it," Trinculo said. "We steal by a plumb line and a carpenter's level. We steal properly and according to the rules, as I hope that your grace will agree."

"I thank you for that jest," Stephano said. "Here's a garment for it. Wit shall not go unrewarded while I am King of this country. 'Steal by line and level' is an excellent sally of wit; there's another garment for it."

Trinculo said, "Monster, come, put some sticky lime upon your fingers so that you have the sticky fingers of a thief, and carry away the rest of the clothing."

"I want nothing to do with that clothing," Caliban said. "We shall lose our opportunity to kill the magician, and we shall all be turned into barnacles or into apes with villainously low foreheads."

People in this culture believed that barnacles were a kind of geese that began life as shellfish.

Stephano ordered, "Monster, get to working with your fingers. Help to bear this clothing away to where my barrel of wine is, or I'll fire you and turn you out of my kingdom."

He handed Caliban a garment and said, "Come on, carry this."

Trinculo added another garment and said, "And carry this."

Stephano added a third garment and said, "And this."

A noise of hunters sounded. Several spirits in the form of hunting hounds chased after Caliban, Stephano, and Trinculo.

Prospero and Ariel encouraged the dogs to chase the thieves.

"Hey, Mountain, hey!" Prospero shouted.

Ariel shouted, "Silver! There it goes, Silver!"

"Fury, Fury! There, Tyrant, there! Listen! Hark!" Prospero shouted.

As Caliban, Stephano, and Trinculo ran away, Prospero said, "Go order my goblins to make sure the thieves' joints convulse painfully. Tell my goblins to make the thieves' sinews grow shorter with the cramps of old people, and torment the thieves and cause bruises until they are more spotted than a panther or mountain cat."

"Listen to them roar with fright!" Ariel said.

"Let them be hunted soundly," Prospero said. "Now, all my enemies are at my mercy. My labors shall end shortly, and you, Ariel, shall freely fly in the air. For just a little while longer, serve me and obey my commands."

CHAPTER 5

— 5.1 —

Prospero said to Ariel, "Now does my plan gather to a head. My charms work, my spirits obey, and time is not burdened by too many remaining tasks. What time is it?"

"Soon it will be six o'clock," Ariel answered. "At six, my Lord, you said our work should cease."

"I did say so, when I first caused the tempest. Say, my spirit, how are the King and his followers?"

"They are confined together just as you ordered and just as you left them. They are all prisoners, sir, in the grove of lime trees that shelters your dwelling from the weather. They cannot budge until you release them. The King, his brother, and your brother, are all three out of their wits, and the other Lords are mourning over them, full of sorrow and dismay. The chief mourner is the man whom, sir, you called 'the good old Lord Gonzalo.' His tears run down his beard, like drops of winter water from the melting ice on eaves of reeds and thatched roofs. Your spells so strongly work on them that if you now saw them, you would pity them and feel sorry for them."

"Do you think so, spirit?" Prospero asked.

"I would pity them and feel sorry for them, sir, were I human," Ariel replied.

"And I shall do the same. You are an airy spirit, yet you have a sense, a feeling, of their afflictions. You are able to feel empathy for them. Shall not I, who am one of their kind, who relishes all as sharply and feels as passionately as they, be kindlier moved than you are? Though I am struck to the quick by their great evils, yet I will side with my noble reason and not with my ignoble fury. It is nobler to show compassion than to take revenge. As long as they repent, I have achieved my purpose and need cause them no further frowns. Go and bring them here, Ariel. My spells on them I will break, their senses I'll restore, and they shall again be themselves."

"I'll fetch them, sir," Ariel said as he flew away.

Alone, Prospero said to himself, "You elves of hills, brooks, lakes without outlets, and groves, and you who on the sands with print-less feet do chase the ebbing Neptune — the sea — and do flee from him when he comes back ... and you small fairies who by Moonlight dance and create the fairy rings of sour grass, whereof the ewe will not bite ... and you whose pastime is to make mushrooms at midnight, who rejoice to hear the solemn evening bell ring curfew ... by the aid of all of you, weaker agents though you be than others, I have bedimmed the Sun at noon, called forth the mutinous winds, and between the green sea and the bright-blue sky set roaring war in the form of a tempest. I have given fire to the dread rattling thunderbolt and split Jove's stout oak with his own weapon. I have made the strongly rooted cliffs shake and by the roots plucked up pine and cedar trees. At my command, graves have awakened their sleepers, opened, and let them go forth because of my very powerful magic art. But this rough magic — these conjuring tricks — I here renounce, and, when I have requested some Heavenly music, which even now I do, to work my end upon their senses that this airy spell is for, I will break my magic staff, bury it a number of fathoms deep in the earth, and deeper than any plummet has plunged I will drown my magic books."

Solemn music began to play, and Prospero used his magic wand to make a circle big enough for several people to stand in.

Ariel returned, leading King Alonso, Sebastian, and Antonio, all of whom were still under Prospero's spell and making frantic gestures as if they were mad. Gonzalo followed King Alonso. Adrian and Francisco and the other Lords followed Gonzalo. All of them entered the circle that Prospero had made.

Prospero said to King Alonso, "Solemn music is the best comforter for an unsettled fancy. It will cure these distracted men here, whose brains, now useless, have been boiled within their skulls!"

He said to all the men in the circle, "All of you men stand here; you have been stopped by my spell."

Prospero said, "Holy Gonzalo, honorable man, my eyes, in sympathy with the appearance of your eyes, drop tears to keep your tears company."

He said to himself, "The spell dissolves quickly, and as the morning steals upon the night, melting the darkness, so their returning senses begin to chase away the fumes that made them ignorant and that clouded their reason that is now clearing. They will quickly return to their senses."

He added, "Oh, good Gonzalo, my true preserver, you saved my life and the life of my daughter. You are a loyal gentleman to the Lord you follow! I will repay you for your virtuous actions; I will do so both with words and deeds."

Prospero said to King Alonso, "Most cruelly did you, King Alonso, treat me and my daughter. Your brother, Sebastian, was an accessory."

He said to Sebastian, "You are now punished for your evil actions, Sebastian."

He said to his brother, Antonio, "Flesh and blood, you, my brother, welcomed ambition, expelled pity and natural feeling. You, with Sebastian, whose inward evil is strongest, would here have killed your King. I forgive you, unnatural though you are."

He said to himself, "Their understanding begins to swell and grow, and the approaching tide of understanding will shortly fill the shores of reason that now lie foul and muddy. But not one of them who looks at me now would recognize me because of the way I am dressed."

He said, "Ariel, fetch me the hat and rapier in my dwelling. I will take off my magician's cloak and I will put on the clothing I habitually dressed in when I was Duke of Milan. Quickly, spirit. You shall before long be free."

Prospero took off his magician's robe, and Ariel returned with a hat and a sword and helped him dress.

As he helped Prospero dress, Ariel sang this song:

"Where the bee sucks, there suck I:

"In a cowslip's bell I lie;

"There I rest when owls do cry.

"On the bat's back I do fly

"Pursuing summer merrily.

"Merrily, merrily shall I live now

"Under the blossom that hangs on the bough."

Prospero said, "Why, that's my dainty Ariel! I shall miss you. But you shall have freedom; indeed, you will. Go to the King's ship, invisible as you are. There you shall find the sailors asleep under the hatches. Awaken the Captain and the

Boatswain and compel them to come to this place. Do this immediately, please."

"I drink the air before me the way that mortals devour the road," Ariel said, "and I will return before your pulse beats twice."

Ariel flew quickly away.

Gonzalo came out of the spell first and said, "All torment, trouble, wonder, and amazement can be found here. May some Heavenly power guide us out of this terrifying country!"

The others regained their senses.

Prospero said, "Sir King Alonso, behold me, the wronged Duke of Milan, Prospero. So that you can be assured that a living Prince — not a ghost — does now speak to you, I embrace your body, and to you and your company I bid a hearty welcome."

Prospero hugged King Alonso, who said, "Whether you really are Prospero or you are some magic trick to delude and harm me, I don't know. Your pulse beats as if you are flesh and blood, and since I saw you the affliction of my mind mends. I was insane, but now I am becoming sane again. This calls for, if this is real, a very strange story to explain what has happened. I surrender your Dukedom to you, and I entreat you to pardon me for the wrongs I have done to you. But how is it possible that Prospero is alive on this island?"

Rather than answering King Alonso immediately, Prospero went to Gonzalo and said, "First, noble friend, let me embrace your aged self, whose honor cannot be measured or confined. The respect that I owe to you is limitless."

"Whether this is real or not real, I cannot swear," Gonzalo said. "I simply don't know."

"You still taste some deceptions of the island that will not let you know for certain what is real. Now good things are happening. The deceptions you taste are like elaborate confections made of sugar that depict allegorical figures and scenes. They are sweet deceptions."

Prospero then said, "Welcome, my friends. Welcome, all of you!"

He whispered to Sebastian and Antonio, "But you, my two Lords, be aware that were I so minded, I here and now could make King Alonso your enemy by proving that you are traitors, but at this time I will tell no tales."

Amazed that Prospero could know of Antonio's and his plot to murder the King, Sebastian whispered to Antonio, "The devil has possessed Prospero's body and is speaking."

"No," Prospero said.

He then said to Antonio, "As for you, most wicked sir, whom to call 'brother' would infect my mouth, I forgive your rankest sin; in fact, I forgive all of your sins against me. I also require that you restore my Dukedom to me, which I am sure that you know that you must do. You heard King Alonso."

"If you really are Prospero," King Alonso said, "tell us the details of your preservation. Tell us how you were saved. Tell us how you met us here, who three hours ago were shipwrecked upon this shore, where I have lost — how sharp the stab and the pain of this memory is! — Ferdinand, my dear son."

"I am sorry for it, sir," Prospero said.

"The loss of my son is irreparable, and it is past the cure of even Patience, the goddess of endurance," King Alonso said.

"I think that you have not sought her help," Prospero said. "The goddess' soft grace and aid has helped me with a similar loss. Now I rest peacefully."

Surprised, King Alonso asked, "Have you suffered a similar loss?"

"My loss is as great to me as it is recent," Prospero said. "To bear my great loss, I have weaker means than you do of supporting me because I have lost my daughter."

This is true, Prospero thought. *I have lost my daughter because I will give her away in marriage. King Alonso's son, Ferdinand, of course, is still alive, and King Alonso will gain a daughter through marriage.*

"A daughter?" King Alonso said. "Oh, Heavens, I wish that they were both living in Naples as the King and Queen there! In order to make that happen, I would be willing to lie in that muddy, oozy bed in which my son lies at the bottom of the sea. When did you lose your daughter?"

"In this last tempest," Prospero said.

He added, "I see that these Lords at this meeting have so much to wonder at that they have lost the capacity to reason. They scarcely believe what their eyes are telling them. They wonder whether these words I am speaking come from a mortal man who breathes natural air. They wonder whether I am a spirit."

He said to all the Lords, "Despite the way that your senses have been jostled, know for certain that I am Prospero, the Duke who was thrust out of Milan, who most wonderfully landed on this shore where you were shipwrecked. I then became the ruler of this island.

"I will say no more about this now because it will take days to tell my story. I cannot tell my entire story during a short breakfast, and it is not fitting to tell it at this, our first meeting."

Prospero said to King Alonso, "Welcome, sir. This dwelling is my court. I have a few attendants here and no subjects elsewhere on the island. Please, look here. Because you have given me my Dukedom again, I will give you as good a gift. I will show you a wonder that will make you as happy as the recovery of my Dukedom makes me."

He then pulled aside a curtain and revealed Ferdinand and Miranda playing chess together. Miranda was winning by a large margin.

Miranda said to Ferdinand, "Sweet Lord, you are playing me falsely. You are letting me win."

"I would not play you falsely, my dearest love, for the world," Ferdinand said.

"Well, you should play against me as if you were playing for a score of kingdoms — which is less than the world. You should play to the best of your ability, and even cheat, and if you did cheat, I would say that you are playing fairly. I would be happy to lose on purpose to you just as you are happy to lose on purpose to me."

King Alonso, seeing his son but afraid that he was seeing a spirit, said, "If this vision proves to be an illusion of this island, I shall lose my dear son twice."

Sebastian said, perhaps ironically, "This is a wonderful miracle!"

Ferdinand had been concentrating on Miranda, but when he heard the voices, he looked up, recognized his father, and said, "Though the seas threaten, they are merciful; I have cursed them without cause. My father, whom I thought was dead, is alive."

He knelt before his father to show him respect.

King Alonso said, "Now enjoy all the blessings that a glad father can give to you! Arise, and say how you came here."

Miranda looked at the men — she had never seen so many human beings — and said, "Wonderful! How many good-looking creatures are there here! How beautiful humankind is! Oh, brave and splendid new world, that has such people in it!"

"This is new to you," Prospero said. He knew that many of the men Miranda was looking at had sinned grievously.

"Who is this maiden with whom you were playing chess?" King Alonso asked his son, Ferdinand. "You cannot have known her for longer than three hours. Is she a goddess who separated us and then brought us together again?"

"Sir, she is mortal," Ferdinand said, "but by immortal Providence she's mine. I chose her when I could not ask you, my father, for your advice. At that time, I thought that you were dead. She is the daughter of Prospero, this famous and renowned Duke of Milan, of whom so often I have heard, but never saw before. From him I have received a second life after I nearly drowned, and when I marry his daughter he shall be my second father."

"Then I will be her father-in-law," King Alonso said. "But, oh, how odd will it sound that I must ask my child for forgiveness! I must ask Miranda to forgive me for the way that I have treated her and her father."

"There, sir, stop," Prospero said. "Let us not remember bad events that happened in the past. Both of us will benefit from forgetfulness and forgiveness."

Gonzalo said, "I have wept inwardly, or I would have spoken before now. Look down, you gods, and on this couple drop a blessed crown for it is you who have marked out — as with chalk — the path that brought us here."

King Alonso said, "I say, 'Amen,' Gonzalo!"

Gonzalo said, "Was the Duke of Milan thrust from Milan, so that his descendants would become Kings of Naples? Oh, rejoice beyond a common joy, and engrave this story in gold on lasting pillars. With one voyage, Claribel found her husband at Tunis, and Ferdinand, her brother, found a wife where he himself was lost. Prospero also found his Dukedom on a poor island, and all of us found ourselves when no man was in his own right mind."

King Alonso said to Ferdinand and Miranda, "Give me your hands. Let grief and sorrow always embrace the heart of anyone who does not wish you joy!"

"Let it be so! Amen!" Gonzalo said.

Ariel now returned, leading the ship's Captain and Boatswain.

"Oh, look, sir!" Gonzalo said, "Here are more of us. During the tempest, while we were still on board the ship, I prophesied that if a gallows were anywhere on land, this fellow — the Boatswain — could not drown."

He said to the Boatswain, "Now, blasphemer, who swear so much on ship that you force the grace of God to go overboard, aren't you going to swear on land? Have you no mouth on land? What is the news?"

"The best news is that we have safely found our King and his company; the next best news is that our ship — which, only three hours ago, we thought had been split in two — is as watertight and seaworthy and bravely rigged as when we first put out to sea."

Ariel whispered to Prospero, "Sir, all this service I have done since I left you."

Prospero replied, "My clever little spirit!"

"These events did not happen naturally," King Alonso said, "They increase in strangeness — they grow from strange to stranger. How did you come here?"

The Boatswain replied, "If I did think, sir, I were wide awake, I would try to tell you. We were dead asleep, and — we don't know how — all imprisoned below deck. But just now with strange and several noises of roaring, shrieking, howling, jingling chains, and other kinds of sounds, all of them horrible, we were awakened. Immediately, we were freed. We saw, in all her trim, our royal, good, and gallant ship, and our Captain danced with joy to see her. In an instant, as if in a dream, the Captain and I were separated from the other sailors and were dazedly brought here."

Ariel whispered to Prospero, "Was it well done?"

"Splendidly, my diligent spirit," Prospero replied. "You shall be free."

"This is as strange a maze as ever men walked and there is in this business more than nature can account for," King Alonso said. "Some oracle of the gods must give us the knowledge we now lack."

"Sir, my liege," Prospero said, "do not trouble your mind by thinking about the strangeness of this business. When we have leisure time, which shall be soon, I will tell you what you want to know about everything that has happened here. You will be satisfied with my explanation, which will not need the help of an oracle. Until then, be cheerful and be happy with the events that have occurred."

Prospero whispered to Ariel, "Come here, spirit. Set Caliban and his companions free; untie the spell that binds them."

Ariel flew away.

Prospero said to King Alonso, "How are you, my gracious sir? There are yet missing from your company some few odd lads whom you have not remembered."

Ariel returned, driving before him Caliban, Stephano, and Trinculo, the last two of whom were wearing rich clothing that they had stolen.

Stephano said, "Let every man look after all the rest, and let no man look after himself, for all is only fortune and luck. Have courage, gallant monster, have courage!"

"If the eyes I wear in my head truly see what they seem to see, this is a welcome sight," Trinculo said.

"Oh, Setebos, who is my god," Caliban said, "these are splendid spirits indeed! How fine my master is! I am afraid that he will chastise me."

Sebastian laughed at the three newcomers and said, "What things are these, Antonio? Will money buy them?"

"Most likely," Antonio replied. "One of them resembles a plain fish, and is, no doubt, marketable."

"Look at the cloth badges these two men are wearing, my Lords," Prospero said. "Most badges worn by servants are the insignia that tell whose servants they are, but in this case the badges are stolen clothing. Can you look at these badges and say that these men are honest?

"This third one, a misshapen knave, had a witch for his mother. She was so strong that she could control the Moon, make the sea flow and ebb, and command the tides to ignore the Moon's power. These three have robbed me, and this demi-devil — for he is a bastard whose father was a devil — had plotted with them to murder me. Two of these fellows you know; they traveled here with you. This thing of darkness belongs to this island."

Caliban said, "I shall be painfully pinched to death."

King Alonso said, "Isn't this man Stephano, my drunken butler?"

"He is drunk," Sebastian said. "Where did he find wine?"

King Alonso said, "And Trinculo is drunk enough to dance a reel. Where did they find this grand liquor that has flushed their faces?"

He asked Trinculo, "How did you come to be in this pickle?"

"The pickle I am in is both a predicament and a preserving agent, as in pickled cucumbers," Trinculo said. "I have been in such a pickle — a dank and dirty and stinking pool of water — since I saw you last that, I am afraid, I will never get the pickling preservative out of my bones. Flies will ignore my body after I die."

"How are you doing, Stephano?" Sebastian asked.

"Don't touch me! I am not Stephano any more! I am nothing but a painful cramp!"

"So you would be King of the island, pally?" Prospero asked, sarcastically.

"I should have been a sore King then — both a sore-y — that is, sorry — King and a King with sores," Stephano replied.

King Alonso pointed at Caliban and said, "This is as strange a thing as I have ever looked at."

"He is as disproportioned in his manners as in his shape," Prospero said.

He said to Caliban, "Go to my dwelling, and take with you your companions. If you want to have my pardon, decorate it handsomely."

"Yes, that I will," Caliban replied, "and I'll be wise hereafter and seek your grace. What a thrice-double ass was I to take this drunkard for a god and worship this dull fool!"

"Go now!" Prospero ordered. "Away!"

King Alonso told Stephano and Trinculo, "Go, and put your rich clothing back where you found it."

"Or stole it, rather," Sebastian said.

Caliban, Stephano, and Trinculo left to obey their orders.

This was the first time that Caliban had been allowed in Prospero's dwelling since Caliban had tried to rape Miranda. Like Ariel, Caliban would soon be free.

Prospero said to King Alonso, "Sir, I invite your Highness and your followers to enter my poor dwelling, where you shall take your rest for this one night, part of which I will spend telling you things that, I don't doubt, shall make the evening pass quickly. I will tell you the story of my life and the events that have happened since I came to this island. In the morning, I will take you to your ship and then we shall travel to Naples, where I hope to see the wedding of these our dearly beloved children solemnized. Then I will go to my Milan, where my every third thought shall be about my grave."

"I long to hear the story of your life, which must sound strange to the ear," King Alonso said.

"I will tell you everything," Prospero said, "and I promise you calm seas and auspicious winds. We will sail so quickly that we shall catch up with your royal fleet, which is now far away."

Prospero whispered to Ariel, "My Ariel, chick, this is your final order: Ensure good weather for sailing. Then return to the elements and be free, and fare you well!"

Prospero said to his guests, "Please go inside my dwelling."

EPILOGUE

Prospero remained outside his dwelling to say these words to you, the readers of this book:

"Now my spells are all overthrown,
"And what strength I have is my own,
"Which is most faint. Now, it is true,
"I must be here confined by you,
"Or sent to Naples. Let me not,
"Since I have my Dukedom got
"And pardoned the deceiver, dwell
"On this bare island because of your spell;
"But release me from my binding bands
"With the help of your good hands —
"Applaud me in your minds.
"And write reviews online that say this book is fine.
"Gentle breath and praise of yours my sails
"Must fill, or else my project fails,
"Which was to please. Now I lack
"Spirits to command, art to enchant,
"And my ending is despair —
"Unless I be relieved by my prayer,
"Which pierces so that it assaults
"Mercy itself and frees all faults.
"As you from crimes would pardoned be,
"Let your indulgence set me free."

Appendix A: About the Author

It was a dark and stormy night. Suddenly a cry rang out, and on a hot summer night in 1954, Josephine, wife of Carl Bruce, gave birth to a boy — me. Unfortunately, this young married couple allowed Reuben Saturday, Josephine's brother, to name their first-born. Reuben, aka "The Joker," decided that Bruce was a nice name, so he decided to name me Bruce Bruce. I have gone by my middle name — David — ever since.

Being named Bruce David Bruce hasn't been all bad. Bank tellers remember me very quickly, so I don't often have to show an ID. It can be fun in charades, also. When I was a counselor as a teenager at Camp Echoing Hills in Warsaw, Ohio, a fellow counselor gave the signs for "sounds like" and "two words," then she pointed to a bruise on her leg twice. Bruise Bruise? Oh yeah, Bruce Bruce is the answer!

Uncle Reuben, by the way, gave me a haircut when I was in kindergarten. He cut my hair short and shaved a small bald spot on the back of my head. My mother wouldn't let me go to school until the bald spot grew out again.

Of all my brothers and sisters (six in all), I am the only transplant to Athens, Ohio. I was born in Newark, Ohio, and have lived all around Southeastern Ohio. However, I moved to Athens to go to Ohio University and have never left.

At Ohio U, I never could make up my mind whether to major in English or Philosophy, so I got a bachelor's degree with a double major in both areas, then I added a master's degree in English and a master's degree in Philosophy.

Currently, and for a long time to come (I eat fruits and vegetables), I am spending my retirement writing books such as *Nadia Comaneci: Perfect 10*, *The Funniest People in Dance*, *Homer's* Iliad: *A Retelling in Prose*, and *William Shakespeare's* Macbeth: *A Retelling in Prose*.

By the way, my sister Brenda Kennedy writes romances such as *A New Beginning* and *Shattered Dreams*.

Appendix B: Some Books by David Bruce

Retellings of a Classic Work of Literature

Arden of Faversham: *A Retelling*

Ben Jonson's The Alchemist: *A Retelling*

Ben Jonson's The Arraignment, or Poetaster: *A Retelling*

Ben Jonson's Bartholomew Fair: *A Retelling*

Ben Jonson's The Case is Altered: *A Retelling*

Ben Jonson's Catiline's Conspiracy: *A Retelling*

Ben Jonson's The Devil is an Ass: *A Retelling*

Ben Jonson's Epicene: *A Retelling*

Ben Jonson's Every Man in His Humor: *A Retelling*

Ben Jonson's Every Man Out of His Humor: *A Retelling*

Ben Jonson's The Fountain of Self-Love, or Cynthia's Revels: *A Retelling*

Ben Jonson's The Magnetic Lady, or Humors Reconciled: *A Retelling*

Ben Jonson's The New Inn, or The Light Heart: *A Retelling*

Ben Jonson's Sejanus' Fall: *A Retelling*

Ben Jonson's The Staple of News: *A Retelling*

Ben Jonson's A Tale of a Tub: *A Retelling*

Ben Jonson's Volpone, or the Fox: *A Retelling*

Christopher Marlowe's Complete Plays: Retellings

Christopher Marlowe's Dido, Queen of Carthage: *A Retelling*

Christopher Marlowe's Doctor Faustus: *Retellings of the 1604 A-Text and of the 1616 B-Text*

Christopher Marlowe's Edward II: *A Retelling*

Christopher Marlowe's The Massacre at Paris: *A Retelling*

Christopher Marlowe's The Rich Jew of Malta: *A Retelling*

Christopher Marlowe's Tamburlaine, Parts 1 and 2: *Retellings*

Dante's Divine Comedy: *A Retelling in Prose*

Dante's Inferno: *A Retelling in Prose*

Dante's Purgatory: *A Retelling in Prose*

Dante's Paradise: *A Retelling in Prose*

The Famous Victories of Henry V: *A Retelling*

From the Iliad *to the* Odyssey: *A Retelling in Prose of Quintus of Smyrna's* Posthomerica

George Chapman, Ben Jonson, and John Marston's Eastward Ho! *A Retelling*

George Peele's The Arraignment of Paris: *A Retelling*

George Peele's The Battle of Alcazar: *A Retelling*

George Peele's David and Bathsheba, and the Tragedy of Absalom: *A Retelling*

George Peele's Edward I: *A Retelling*

George Peele's The Old Wives' Tale: *A Retelling*

George-a-Greene: *A Retelling*

The History of King Leir: *A Retelling*

Homer's Iliad: *A Retelling in Prose*

Homer's Odyssey: *A Retelling in Prose*

J.W. Gent.'s The Valiant Scot: *A Retelling*

Jason and the Argonauts: A Retelling in Prose of Apollonius of Rhodes' Argonautica

John Ford: Eight Plays Translated into Modern English

John Ford's The Broken Heart: *A Retelling*

John Ford's The Fancies, Chaste and Noble: *A Retelling*

John Ford's The Lady's Trial: *A Retelling*

John Ford's The Lover's Melancholy: *A Retelling*

John Ford's Love's Sacrifice: *A Retelling*

John Ford's Perkin Warbeck: *A Retelling*

John Ford's The Queen: *A Retelling*

John Ford's 'Tis Pity She's a Whore: *A Retelling*

John Lyly's Campaspe: *A Retelling*

John Lyly's Endymion, The Man in the Moon: *A Retelling*

John Lyly's Galatea: *A Retelling*

John Lyly's Love's Metamorphosis: *A Retelling*

John Lyly's Midas: *A Retelling*

John Lyly's Mother Bombie: *A Retelling*

John Lyly's Sappho and Phao: *A Retelling*

John Lyly's The Woman in the Moon: *A Retelling*

John Webster's The White Devil: *A Retelling*

King Edward III: *A Retelling*

Mankind: *A Medieval Morality Play (A Retelling)*

Margaret Cavendish's The Unnatural Tragedy: *A Retelling*

The Merry Devil of Edmonton: *A Retelling*

The Summoning of Everyman: *A Medieval Morality Play (A Retelling)*

Robert Greene's Friar Bacon and Friar Bungay: *A Retelling*

The Taming of a Shrew: *A Retelling*

Tarlton's Jests: A Retelling

Thomas Middleton's A Chaste Maid in Cheapside: *A Retelling*

Thomas Middleton's Women Beware Women: *A Retelling*

Thomas Middleton and Thomas Dekker's The Roaring Girl: *A Retelling*

Thomas Middleton and William Rowley's The Changeling: *A Retelling*

The Trojan War and Its Aftermath: Four Ancient Epic Poems

Virgil's Aeneid: *A Retelling in Prose*

William Shakespeare's 5 Late Romances: Retellings in Prose

William Shakespeare's 10 Histories: Retellings in Prose

William Shakespeare's 11 Tragedies: Retellings in Prose

William Shakespeare's 12 Comedies: Retellings in Prose

William Shakespeare's 38 Plays: Retellings in Prose

William Shakespeare's 1 Henry IV, aka Henry IV, Part 1: *A Retelling in Prose*

William Shakespeare's 2 Henry IV, aka Henry IV, Part 2: *A Retelling in Prose*

William Shakespeare's 1 Henry VI, aka Henry VI, Part 1: *A Retelling in Prose*

William Shakespeare's 2 Henry VI, aka Henry VI, Part 2: *A Retelling in Prose*

William Shakespeare's 3 Henry VI, aka Henry VI, Part 3: *A Retelling in Prose*

William Shakespeare's All's Well that Ends Well: *A Retelling in Prose*

William Shakespeare's Antony and Cleopatra: *A Retelling in Prose*

William Shakespeare's As You Like It: *A Retelling in Prose*

William Shakespeare's The Comedy of Errors: *A Retelling in Prose*

William Shakespeare's Coriolanus: *A Retelling in Prose*

William Shakespeare's Cymbeline: *A Retelling in Prose*

William Shakespeare's Hamlet: *A Retelling in Prose*

William Shakespeare's Henry V: *A Retelling in Prose*

William Shakespeare's Henry VIII: *A Retelling in Prose*

William Shakespeare's Julius Caesar: *A Retelling in Prose*

William Shakespeare's King John: *A Retelling in Prose*

William Shakespeare's King Lear: *A Retelling in Prose*

William Shakespeare's Love's Labor's Lost: *A Retelling in Prose*

William Shakespeare's Macbeth: *A Retelling in Prose*

William Shakespeare's Measure for Measure: *A Retelling in Prose*

William Shakespeare's The Merchant of Venice: *A Retelling in Prose*

William Shakespeare's The Merry Wives of Windsor: *A Retelling in Prose*

William Shakespeare's A Midsummer Night's Dream: *A Retelling in Prose*

William Shakespeare's Much Ado About Nothing: *A Retelling in Prose*

William Shakespeare's Othello: *A Retelling in Prose*

William Shakespeare's Pericles, Prince of Tyre: *A Retelling in Prose*

William Shakespeare's Richard II: *A Retelling in Prose*

William Shakespeare's Richard III: *A Retelling in Prose*

William Shakespeare's Romeo and Juliet: *A Retelling in Prose*

William Shakespeare's The Taming of the Shrew: *A Retelling in Prose*

William Shakespeare's The Tempest: *A Retelling in Prose*

William Shakespeare's Timon of Athens: *A Retelling in Prose*

William Shakespeare's Titus Andronicus: *A Retelling in Prose*

William Shakespeare's Troilus and Cressida: *A Retelling in Prose*

William Shakespeare's Twelfth Night: *A Retelling in Prose*

William Shakespeare's The Two Gentlemen of Verona: *A Retelling in Prose*

William Shakespeare's The Two Noble Kinsmen: *A Retelling in Prose*

William Shakespeare's The Winter's Tale: *A Retelling in Prose*